# THE
# STARS
# GLEAM
# BRIGHTER

# THE STARS GLEAM BRIGHTER

BENITA J. PRINS

Copyright © 2021 by Benita J. Prins

ISBN 978-1988615196

*Previously published as* Starscape.

Cover & interior design by Benita J. Prins
Kairos Book Design & Editing | kairosbookdesign.com

First paperback printing, June 2015
Third edition, May 2021

To
DAD, MUM, JAMES, ELIZABETH, THERESA,
GERALD, STEPHEN, JOSEPH, ANTHONY, and
PHILIP
and to
RACHEL, HANNAH, and LEAH
but especially to
BRIDGET
because you happen to be responsible for this
book's existence.

# PROLOGUE

A LEGEND THAT TELLS OF A STAR... MORE BEAUTIFUL THAN any other... even before the sun... thousands of years ago... wiser than the wisest of men... a song of unearthly beauty...

Royaleisia.

The star disappeared from the heavens, but if you go to the Northern Mountains, you can hear its song, still echoing from peak to lofty peak. The keenest-eyed people have claimed to have seen her, standing in the clear, moonlit night air, her arms stretched to the sky.

They have claimed that it is Royaleisia herself, and that she will in time come to avert the danger which will threaten Militer. They say that when the peril is at last passed away, there will come a song.

A song that is great and clear, heartrending and pure, so lovely that men would die for it.

The story may not be true – it may be some evil scheming of Jalavak's, but people go to the Northern Mountains, as I have told you.

The meaning of Royaleisia – the Strong.

# 1

It was just dawn. The early morning sun shone brightly on the Malarn Lake. The rays pierced the shadows in every hollow of the surrounding meadows. A few clouds swam lazily through the deep blue sky.

Ringard looked up at the sun. It did not hurt his eyes – no light was too bright for the eyes of the Startern people. Ringard was a Startern; but though his home was in Staran with King Kanethon and his kin, he and his brother Pluriel had lived here in Fortaer for some years. Ringard was tall and slender, with dark eyes and hair that was blacker than black: the typical Startern colouring.

Now as he looked a cloud passed over the sun, a grey cloud, dark grey. He shivered slightly. A few light drops of rain fell. With a worried look in his face he turned and entered the city.

Serpent's Road was a distasteful area of the city of Malarn, where pickpockets prowled the bustling marketplace and foreigners jabbered in strange tongues. Still, the Silver Spear Inn was well-kept and a pleasant enough place to eat dinner of an evening.

Ringard rang the bell on the counter, then turned around and surveyed the common room as he waited for Galdore to come. Most of the patrons of the Silver Spear were townsfolk, but today there were a few Gausher, from the land of Gaush across the mountains.

"What can we get for you today?"

Galdore, the twenty-three-year-old innkeeper, had taken over the running of the inn when his father had died a year ago. He was a generally gentle-spoken young man in keeping with his shoulder-length gold hair and dark blue eyes, but no one had tried to cheat him since a seedy stranger had attempted to do so five months earlier. Galdore had beaten the Gausher soundly; the vanquished thief had slunk off to one of the poorer taverns of Malarn.

"The usual, please, Galdore," Ringard replied.

"That would be baked chicken with a mug of ale? If you'll find yourself a seat, I'll send Tristal round directly."

"*Samach ne*," Ringard thanked Galdore as he made for an empty table in the far corner of the room.

As he waited for his food, Ringard listened to the rumours circulating the room. One working-class fellow was telling his friend about strange shadows he'd seen in the town square on his way home the previous night. Apparently these shadows had moved about the square with nothing to cast them. Another troublemaker informed anyone who would listen that the governor of the city of Forran, King Leftar's nephew Eparne, was conspiring to overthrow his uncle. Some of the ideas put forth were so ridiculous that Ringard was hard put not to laugh aloud.

A few minutes passed before Tristal arrived.

He was Galdore's brother, two years younger, but could have been his twin as far as looks went. Tristal was carrying a platter loaded with fragrant chicken, potatoes, and beans, plus a quart of ale. Ringard dropped two copper pennies into the young man's hand.

"It smells delicious, as usual."

As Ringard ate his dinner, a cloaked figure slid into the seat across from him.

"Pluriel! There you are at last. I was beginning to wonder what had happened to you."

"Sorry I'm late, but I came as soon as I could. I overheard something as I came through the market after speaking with King Leftar. I believe it could be important."

Ringard swallowed his mouthful. "Go ahead, tell me."

"I expect you don't remember the prophecy of the Great Seer regarding the Sword of the Star?"

Ringard shook his head.

"'When the Star falls from the sky, the Sword of the Star shall be restored,'" Pluriel half-chanted. His brother looked up.

"You remember the tale about the theft of the Sword of the Star from the Golden Palace – how the minions of Jalavak broke in by night and took the ancient sword, secreting it in Duskmoor Keep."

"Yes, I recall that," Ringard said. "But what can the first part of the prophecy mean? 'When the Star falls from the sky.' It makes no sense. To which star does it refer? And how is it possible for a star to fall from the sky?"

"Royaleisia," muttered Pluriel, looking around to make sure no one was near enough to hear what he said. The room was beginning to empty out, however, and they enjoyed a little more privacy. A few dishes clattered as Tristal cleared a vacated table nearby.

Ringard paused for a moment before replying. Then he nodded slowly. "You believe the legends and peasants' tales?"

"Yes, I do." Pluriel shoved his chair back and stood up, looking down at his brother. "I am going to the Nevarra Swamp to make an attempt at recovering the Sword. You know it's the only weapon with which Jalavak can be defeated. Well, if we can get it back, then we have a chance of finally ending his reign over the South. Will you come with me, brother?"

"Of course I'll come with you!" Ringard

exclaimed. "Do you think I'd let you face the dragon-keeper alone?"

Pluriel laughed, releasing some tension from his face. "I don't know that it's actually a *dragon* that guards the Sword, but I'll be glad of your company in any event."

As Pluriel reseated himself, two mugs of ale slid across the table and the other two chairs scraped back.

"How is your meal?" asked Galdore. "I trust you are not disappointed?"

Ringard shook his head. "It's very good, just as I expected."

"I'm glad," Galdore replied. "But Tristal says we may be able to give you more than just your supper."

"What do you mean?" Pluriel asked, looking suspiciously from Galdore to Tristal. "In what would we need help?"

Galdore smiled. "No fear, we're friends of yours and foes of Jalavak's. My brother was telling me that you two were discussing the possibility of recovering the Sword of the Star."

"What is it to you?" questioned Pluriel.

"We wish to serve our King and help to end the tyranny of Jalavak. If you intend to go to

Nevarra, we will go with you – if you permit it."

Ringard looked to Pluriel. "I would accept their offer, but this is your idea."

Pluriel turned a discerning stare on Galdore and Tristal. "What's your purpose in wanting to join us?"

Tristal shrugged. "Nothing more than what Galdore has told you." He flashed a brief smile. "Although I have always had a wish to do great things for Fortaer."

Settling back against the wall, Pluriel sat in silence for some time, his eyes closed. Finally he opened them and grinned. "I suppose it's all right. But," he continued, his smile disappearing, "you understand the danger. We may well not return."

The resolution on their faces did not waver. "We are coming with you no matter what," Tristal stated.

Pluriel smiled again. "I'll speak with the King tomorrow. Any such expedition would have to be undertaken with his prior approval."

"It's an interesting idea," said the King, staring

out the window, "but I'm not at all convinced it's a good one. First, it's based on conjecture. You are only assuming that this prophecy could be about to come true. And I hardly like to risk you and Ringard on a mere conjecture. The thing would be extremely risky. If the legends speak true, then the keeper of the Sword is a dragon, old and wily. That is assuming," he continued, turning around, "that  you could reach the Nevarra Swamp safely in the first place. Jalavak has watchful eyes in all lands."

"I'm sure we could reach the Swamp easily enough. The main problem would be find the Sword, of course." Pluriel seemed about to go on, but King Leftar had turned back to the window and was no longer paying much attention.

A long and uncomfortable silence ensued, during which Pluriel stood awkwardly staring at the King's back. Finally the monarch looked round again and spoke one word.

"No."

Pluriel started. He hadn't been expecting Leftar to speak just then, and the terse dismissal of his request startled him further.

"No?" he questioned stupidly.

"No," repeated the King. "It's too dangerous.

You and your brother are too helpful here for me to let you go on a suicide journey. I would be insane to do so."

He made a curt gesture with his hand, signalling that the audience was over. Pluriel opened his mouth one more time, but closed it with a sigh before any words came out. He backed out of the chamber, then strode down the hall, his angry footsteps fading away.

King Leftar tapped his empty goblet sharply on the table. *Tap tap tap, tap TAP tap.* He couldn't get that stupid prophecy out of his mind. Stupid? All right, not stupid; prophets' words were inspired by Elamm'. It was the fact that Pluriel and his brother wanted to leave Fortaer that disturbed him.

*You can't keep them forever*, he reminded himself. Yet surely he had given Pluriel the right answer.

"Uncle?"

*Not Eparne again. Not now.* The King smiled tightly. "Come in, Eparne."

His nephew sauntered in. "Something the

matter?"

Well, he didn't like Eparne, but he needed to talk this out with someone. "Pluriel Frosindalon wants to go look for the Sword."

"Of the Star?"

"Exactly."

"And you said yes, of course?" Was that a slight gleam in Eparne's eye? No. Of course not. Eparne was nigh a brother to the Frosindalion.

"I said no," the King stated tersely, filling his goblet and taking a good sip.

"Why's that?" queried Eparne, pouring himself some wine uninvited.

Leftar laughed, humourlessly. "Perhaps because Ringard and Pluriel happen to be two of my best advisers?"

"Yeees..." drawled Eparne, drawing out the word. "But, you know, if they could get the Sword for you, you would possess the immediate advantage over Jalavak. An advantage, forgive me, which I think you sorely need."

Leftar looked up and thought for a moment. "I could send someone to the Swamp, I suppose," he said hesitantly. "Perhaps – "

"You can't send just anyone, uncle," Eparne cut in. "It has to be someone you can trust. If I were you, I would choose the Frosindalion. Ringard and Pluriel are your best chance."

The King hesitated for a time. Then he shook his head.

Eparne continued to make his case. *Can the boy never leave others' affairs alone?* "They could make the trip in three months or less," he pushed.

"They could also be killed in the doing of it," Leftar pointed out testily.

"Oh, it's a slight possibility, but very unlikely, you know. Pluriel is one of Fortaer's foremost swordsmen, and Ringard is not far behind in prowess." *Isn't that the precise reason I'm reluctant to let them go?* "I think it would be quite safe if they were to find a few friends to go with them."

He stared at the King. Leftar thought carefully for some time, weighing in his mind all possible outcomes of his decision either way. Finally he nodded.

"Summon Pluriel back."

# 2

"SHE BEAT YOU ONCE MORE, EH?" ROMAGNA GENTLY sponged the welts on Eloderaẏ's hands. "That woman should be given her own back."

Eloderaẏ bit her lip and didn't reply.

"What did she accuse you of this time?"

"Stealing," whispered Eloderaẏ.

"Did you tell her the truth? No, don't answer that. I can see you didn't."

"It wouldn't have helped, and Neltan is only five."

"Like I said, Mistress Stellatin should be given her own back. Let her take that child's place, slaving and starving."

Eloderaý cringed as Romagna wrapped the bandages around.

"Sorry."

"S'okay," she muttered, gritting her teeth. *It could be worse.* She repeated herself aloud. "I've seen worse."

"I know you have," growled Romagna. "What I could do to that woman."

Eloderaý shook her head just as a small form shot through the kitchen door and halted, panting, before her.

"Ree, they're coming for you!"

"Who?"

Neltan gasped for breath. "Soldiers!"

"What?" Eloderaý grasped the boy by the shoulders, heedless of the protest in her hands.

"Mistress Stellatin sent for them. I heard her! She said – " He paused, trying to catch his breath. "She said you were a thief as should be hanged!"

The two girls were utterly silent, staring at each other. Then Romagna awoke into action.

"Eloderaý, you're to go. You're to run, and never come back. Have you anything you need?"

"No?" She was dazed; she couldn't follow what was going on. Was 'no' the right answer?

"East. Go east. You should leave Tralaga entirely."

"What!" she exclaimed, suddenly waking up.

"They'll look for you throughout the land. You should go to Staran, maybe Fortaer, maybe even Gaush. No, not Gaush, they'll think of it. Staran, they won't think you could cross the Highlands alive."

Eloderaý nodded. Tears popped into her eyes, making everything blurry again. "Romagna, I'll miss you."

The other girl hugged her quickly, and Eloderaý knelt down to embrace Neltan. "You're wonderful, Neltan. If it weren't for you..." She shut her mouth. ...*I'd be dead.* He was only five. "I'll miss you too."

"Aww..." He wormed out of her arms. "Just go, okay?"

Romagna's expression agreed with the child. "The soldiers are fast. We all know that."

"Thanks. Both of you."

"Don't take the road!" Romagna called after her.

"*Hana-gawë?*"

The greeting sounded almost like a question to Gydi, who swung around, startled. He saw a young man, auburn hair curling on his shoulders, blue eyes peering enquiringly out of a pinched thin face. He looked delicate, and his attitude was slightly nervous, as if he were afraid of being punished for the smallest offence.

"*Hana-gawë*; welcome to the Travellers' Home," Gydi replied. "And what might I do for you, young fellow?"

The boy did not relax, despite Gydi's cheerful greeting. He laid his hands, palms up, on the counter, and Gydi glanced at them with a frown. Both were bound tightly with strips of bandage.

"Are you all right there?"

The boy's cheeks flamed and he yanked his hands out of sight. "I have no money," he stated. His voice had not yet broken and sounded as timid as the thin face looked.

Gydi looked closely at the boy. "Your accent. You're not from here," he deduced. "Kefield, maybe? Or Faerbek?"

A look of what seemed to be fear crossed the boy's face. "It isn't your business where I'm from," he said defiantly.

"Calm down, boy," the innkeeper reassured him. "I just find it interesting, all the different places my guests hail from."

"I'm not here as a guest. Like I told you, I've got no money. Would you employ me for a few weeks? I can sleep in the stable if you like, and I'll eat the scraps. Just please, I need food for my journey."

Gydi became even more curious. The young man sounded desperate. "What's this journey?"

"That's none of your business either."

"But if I'm going to employ you, I need to know something of you, boy. I can't hire just anyone who comes my way looking for work."

The desperate look on the boy's face turned sullen. "I have to go to Staran. Or something. As long as it's not in Tralaga."

"What's with our land?"

"Bored of it." He was answering the questions, sure, but the boy wasn't going to say anything more than was absolutely necessary.

"And your name?"

The boy paused for the shortest second before replying. "Kylyn."

Gydi leaned in to get a closer look at Kylyn. His eyes narrowed a little, then he spoke.

"I'll give you work waiting on tables and clearing the dirty dishes. I've got lots of guests right now and no help. You can sleep in the stable like you suggested, and at the end of two weeks I'll give you food enough to reach Tímil. You can eat leftovers for now. My name's Gydi."

Kylyn's face brightened considerably.

"Thank you so much, Gydi!"

Mustn't seem overly kind. "Well, get started then, boy! There's someone finished over there; go clear what he's left."

As the boy ran off, Gydi's brow furrowed. No question about it, none at all. That boy was strange. Wouldn't say where he was from – though his accent suggested Kefield – was leaving Tralaga, didn't care where he went, and the name he'd said was definitely false if you considered that pause before he said it. Gydi might almost have taken Kylyn for a girl if he'd heard him before he'd seen him. He would take watching and that was a fact.

"They chose the boys from the Silver Spear?"

Ealcar, Captain of the King's Guard, looked confused at King Leftar's consternation.

"Why, yes, my lord. Galdore and Tristal, the sons of the old innkeeper. What was his name again?" Ealcar thought for a moment, but the King was uninterested. He had buried his face in his hands.

"Is something wrong, my lord? Shall I send someone after them to call them back?"

The King shook his head but didn't look up.

*Of all the men in Malarn whom he could have found, Pluriel had to take* them?

# 3

THE MOUNTAINS OF FORTAER WERE ONE OF THE MOST majestic sights in all of Militer. Towering as high as two thousand feet into the sky, the range stalked to an end high above the deep blue Tobar Lake. The foursome came in sight of them as they passed along the stream of the Gildan that began high above. Lush grass ran down from the mountains' feet, studded with abundant heartflowers, reaching even here, halfway to Forran.

They made as fast a pace as possible, and by the end of the first day they were exhausted, ready to rest and admire the scenery. The next day would be time enough to cross the Gildan and begin the trek through the Lebon Forest.

"Well, we've gotten this far without mishap," said Tristal as they pitched camp for the night.

"How light-hearted you always appear, Tristal," Ringard said with a smile. "Listening to you, one would think we were on a trip for pleasure!"

Tristal ran through his hair. "Galdore likes to reprove me for that reason," he remarked. "He thinks I'm flippant. But I like to make light of things. Maybe it's my way of whistling in the dark."

"Sometimes it is indeed a good thing to make light of things," agreed Ringard, "but sometimes it is not."

Tristal snorted. "You can't be much over ten, fifteen years older than I, and you give me advice like a father," he teased.

"I'm older than I think you think," Ringard grinned.

"Oh yes? You're thirty, perhaps forty."

Ringard laughed aloud. "A hundred years off the mark, Tristal."

The smirk disappeared from Tristal's face. "You're a hundred and thirty." He stared. "You're having a laugh on me."

"The lifespan of a Startern can reach two hundred and forty-two – at least, that's the longest recorded."

"I thought... oh, great Mountains of Gaush. I thought; well, I knew you were long-lived, but you look young yet..." Tristal stopped and flushed. "I'm rambling."

"We don't age till around a hundred ninety," broke in Pluriel, abruptly pulling Ringard aside. "I feel a threat near us," he murmured. "You and I should watch tonight."

Just after midnight, Pluriel crept through the blackness to wake his brother.

"Nothing has happened yet," he whispered. "But keep alert. I still feel the danger, and my mind is ill at ease."

"My dreams were troubled," replied Ringard, "and I seemed to hear the tramping of heavy feet and the war cries of Flokav. I will not lower my guard."

As Pluriel settled down to sleep, Ringard sat

down a small ways away from the campfire and wrapped his blanket around him. He peered out into the night and immediately seemed to sense unfriendly eyes staring back at him. He saw nothing except the dark shadows of the trees, but his unease continued. He wished he could wake Pluriel, but decided against it. *He is tired. I will wait.*

After a while Ringard's eyes drifted slowly shut. He forced them open, but something that was not weariness gently closed them again. His unease grew until he felt he was choking. *I must stay awake!* Again Ringard opened his eyes, a hard effort this time, only to have them closed yet a third time by some invisible force. He knew that if he allowed himself to doze off for the least minute, none of them would wake again. Somehow he managed to open his eyes one last time.

He looked hard in front of him. The shapes of the trees were the same, but there was something different about the landscape. What was it? He blinked several times. Then he saw.

Before him, earlier, he remembered there had been five trees nearby. The rest were farther back. But now there were – he counted – twelve. Five tall, seven shorter.

Ringard got quietly up. The seven short trees moved.

"Pluriel!"

His warning shout was louder than ever before. His companions leaped up. Galdore and Tristal unsheathed their swords. Pluriel loosed his in its sheath, then took an arrow from his quiver and fit it to his bowstring. With a hideous shriek the seven short trees sprang forward. From the shadows around the camp more Flokav appeared. Pluriel loosed the arrow as Ringard rapidly strung his own bow.

"Stand in a circle, backs to the fire!" yelled Pluriel. Two more of his arrows found their marks in Flokav hearts, then with his next arrow Pluriel stabbed one which leaped at him. Bow abandoned, his sword flashed in the moonlight as he drew it and looked for his friends.

Engaged in fending off several stubborn enemies, Galdore suddenly heard a harsh breathing behind him. Knowing it was not one of his company, he gave an abrupt kick backwards. A shriek and a thud told him his kick had been well-delivered. Now he brought up his sword swiftly to parry a blow from another Flokav. Turning, Galdore served a death blow to the prostrate Flokav whom he'd kicked. Tristal, trained in swordfight like all Fortaeren boys, was faring equally as well as his brother. In fact, he was enjoying the battle as a proof of how well he had absorbed his instructor's endless commands and comments. Ringard, keeping an eye on him, was impressed by the twenty-one-year-old's skill.

With two of Staran's foremost warriors on their enemy's side, the Flokav had little chance despite their advantage in numbers. Around twenty were dead when the rest gave up and fled shrieking into the night. Relieved that there were no casualties on their side, the worn out men flung down their weapons and themselves upon the ground, panting.

"Where did they come from?" gasped Galdore when he could speak again. "It was as though they appeared out of nowhere, so suddenly were they there!"

Pluriel's expression was grim. "It shows either that Jalavak is aware of our journey, or that he has grown so bold that he would allow raiding parties to enter Fortaer at will. We'll have to be very cautious as we proceed. From now on, a watch will be set every evening without fail."

# 4

Under the trees of the Lebon Forest, all was perfectly still and silent. From time to time a squirrel chattered at them from the top of a tree, or scuttered through the dried leaves matting the ground, but otherwise there was not a sound. "No sign of any birds," muttered Galdore. "This place is dead."

A sudden harsh hissing noise cut through the silence, and Tristal started violently.

"What in Militer was that?" he cried.

"It was a silisik," muttered Ringard. "There are but few of them in this forest, and I fear we have had the misfortune to run across one of them."

"Are they dangerous?" Galdore asked.

"Usually they eat only small animals such as rabbits, but when one is hungry it will attack people."

Tristal glanced from side to side.

"Don't worry," Pluriel reassured him. "We can manage a small number of them."

"That hardly comforts me," Tristal said under his breath as they continued onwards.

They'd walked for perhaps ten minutes more when another hiss issued from behind a nearby tree, followed quickly by at least five more, all from different directions. Now one of the creatures peered out from its cover. The company caught sight of a long snout before it retreated back into its hiding place once more.

Then a grey body snaked out from behind a different tree. It was long, maybe five feet, and no more than a foot in diameter. Four eyes gleamed white.

"Ugh," exclaimed Galdore involuntarily.

"Draw your swords," instructed Pluriel tensely.

The company stood at the ready as twelve, thirteen, fourteen more of the snake-like creatures appeared from various places. The men and silisiks stared at each other for a few seconds before one of the grey bodies streaked forwards. Pluriel jumped toward it and in one stroke had beheaded it. It fell to the ground and flopped around before lying still. The rest of the silisiks charged as one. For a time the only sounds were those of hissing and striking. Then all was silent once more as the men realised that all the silisiks were dead or had fled.

Galdore dropped his sword and fell on the ground beside it with a slight moan. His brother was at his side in a flash.

"Are you hurt, Galdore? Let me see it!"

"I was bitten near the end," muttered Galdore through clenched teeth.

Ringard quickly knelt beside him. "Oh no," he breathed.

"What's wrong?" Galdore asked him, catching a glimpse of Ringard's face.

"The fangs of a silisik carry a venom which they use to kill their prey," Ringard replied. He looked up at his own brother. "Pluriel, could you find me a heartflower? They're supposed to be abundant in this forest."

Pluriel turned to go.

"Don't move," rasped a voice.

The rest whipped round. Facing Pluriel was a tall Floka wearing an ugly expression on his flat face. Surrounding them all was a group of Flokav, all with drawn bows aimed at the men. The tall Floka made a motion to the Flokav behind him, and four of them laid down their bows and stepped forward.

"You move, we shoot," warned the Floka. The four Flokav grasped the arms of the men. "Up trees," growled the leader, and the travellers were ushered roughly into one tree. More Flokav clambered up after them and bound them to high branches. Then they climbed down and a large guard of Flokav stationed themselves around the tree.

The sky grew dark, and the temperature dropped. Sleep was impossible, though not for the Flokav, to judge from the loud snores below. Galdore quivered and shuddered against the tree limb, his teeth chattering insistently. Ringard struggled out of his cloak, leaned over, as far as the ropes would allow, and dropped it so that it settled over the sick man. He leaned back, and there was a light touch on his shoulder. He started to the alert, but before he could cry out a hand slid over his mouth.

"Hush," hissed a voice.

"Who are you?" Ringard muttered, twisting his head away from the hand.

"I'm here to help you," was the reply, and a knife sawed apart his bonds. He stretched out gratefully as the stranger freed Pluriel and Tristal. When he came to Galdore, however, their rescuer paused. In the moonlight Galdore's face was visible, and it was pale and blotched with red. His mouth hung open and his irregular breathing was laboured. Hastily the newcomer freed him.

Tristal slid forward on his branch and stared at his brother, tears forming in his eyes. "Is he going to die?" he whispered.

The stranger glanced up at Tristal, and his expression was invisible behind a black cloak. Then he returned his gaze to Galdore and began to murmur.

"*Qlehm Elamm' týresrach ren ledh swlrach ren li mhala saranh.*"

Galdore stirred and opened his eyes. The blotches on his face slowly faded to a faint pink, and his pale cheeks returned almost to their natural hue. As strength returned to his body, he struggled to sit up.

"What did you do?" asked Tristal in amazement, but Pluriel and Ringard were looking curiously at the stranger. Pluriel bent over to Ringard and whispered in his ear.

The stranger ignored Tristal's question. "My rope is tied to the next tree over. We can swing over the Flokav's heads on it."

The pink light of dawn was beginning to seep through the branches as the stranger grasped the rope and swung out. As the rope reached its extent, he let go of it and landed lightly some ten feet away from the still-sleeping Flokav. He then tied a rock to the rope as a weight, and swung it back to the others. Tristal caught it and passed it to Galdore.

"Do you think you can make it?" he asked his brother, anxiety remaining clear in his tone.

Galdore nodded. "I don't know what he said, whether it was Jalavak's sorcery or Elamm's blessing. But I feel like my suffering was only a dream!"

"It was no sorcery," Pluriel said as Galdore wrapped his legs around the rope, gripping it tightly, "for he called upon the name of Elamm'."

Galdore pushed himself off the branch and landed close to the stranger. Then he flung the rope back towards the tree, but it fell short by a couple yards, his strength not fully returned. The stranger caught it as it swung back and threw it again. Tristal grabbed it, and he, then Ringard, then Pluriel, swung down to earth.

# 5

BY THE TIME DAY HAD FULLY DAWNED, THE VEILED stranger had led the company far from the Flokav, to the end of the forest. Coming out into the full sunlight, Galdore heaved a sigh of profound relief and lowered himself onto the soft grass.

"Never have I been more grateful for the light of day!"

"I thought our journey was over," admitted Tristal, and Galdore nodded. Ringard was silent, and Pluriel still looked grim.

"It was no coincidence that the Flokav came upon us just then," he said gravely. "I believe they must have been in league with the silisiks, for – "

Tristal interrupted. "Silisiks are just dumb animals – how could they be in league?"

"Jalavak can communicate with beasts and bend them to his will," explained Pluriel. "The jogens, the bear-men, are entirely at his command in all things. I have never heard of silisiks hunting in packs like that, and they rarely attack people unless uncommonly hungry. And small wildlife is still plentiful in the Lebon Forest. Besides, the silisik attack neatly diverted our attention from the approaching Flokav. I'm thankful there are no other forests to pass through on our way to the Nevarra."

They sat in silence for a time, resting. Presently Tristal roused himself and asked the question he'd posed to the stranger earlier.

"How *did* you heal my brother?"

No answer came, and they all looked up. But their rescuer had vanished. Even Pluriel and Ringard's sharp Startern eyesight could detect no sign that he had ever been there.

"How odd!" exclaimed Galdore. "Where can he possibly have got to without our notice?"

Ringard shook his head. "If our conjecture is true, it's no surprise that she – he – can completely vanish without a sound."

"What is your conjecture?" and "Why 'she'?"

asked Galdore and Tristal simultaneously.

Ringard glanced at Pluriel, letting him decide whether or not to disclose their idea.

"Our conjecture is possible but by no means likely," replied Pluriel after a moment, "and I think for now it's best to keep silent regarding it. As for saying 'she', well, could the stranger not have been a woman?"

"I suppose that's true," Galdore agreed after thinking for a few seconds. "In fact, the voice could've been that of a woman, now I think about it. But I suppose we'll never know now."

"Maybe," said Pluriel. "But in any case we should press on with haste. I'm not sure that the Flokav will try to chase us; certainly not before nightfall, and by dusk I wish to be far from here. Our route goes northward now, along the mountains to the Matren Pass."

"I did think," put in Ringard, "that it might be a good idea not to follow along the base of the hills. We could find more cover if we went up into them. But you decide."

"There would be more cover," Pluriel replied thoughtfully. "But now we need all the speed we can muster. Evidently Jalavak knows of our journey somehow, and I doubt not that he will try everything in his power to stop us. I want to reach the Swamp as soon as possible."

As they hiked they talked of many things. Pluriel related to Galdore and Tristal many of Ringard's feats of courage and honour in battle; Ringard flushed at his brother's compliments and in return told tales of Pluriel's own kindness and loyalty to his king. Against much protest from Galdore, Tristal revealed how his brother had once waived a bill that had turned out to be more that a patron could pay. Galdore retaliated by teasing Tristal about his constant joking and fearlessness.

At the end of the day's six-hour march they had reached the bank of the Lazia River. Galdore was given the first watch, but it was an unnecessary precaution that night. The problem which did confront them in the morning was how they should cross the river. They had no boat, and the nearest city was over a day's trek from where they stood. In the end they decided, in the absence of other options, to swim. They stripped off their boots and tunics, stowing them in their packs, and swam the width of the river in shirt and hose. The water was melted snow which came down from the mountains and was yet chill, for it was but early spring.

As they took a brief rest on the other bank,

Tristal pulled a parchment from his pack and studied it. After a while Galdore grew curious and leaned over to see what it was. He exclaimed in surprise.

"*You* have that old map? I was beginning to think a guest must have taken it!"

Tristal laughed but didn't look up. "I should have told you I had it, maybe, but I didn't think you needed it. Look here." He turned the map towards the others. "We have a couple choices going forward. We could go on along the bases of the mountains like we've been doing, and join the Old West Road right where it ascends. Or we could turn northwest now and come to the road in less time. The first route is more direct, but if we take the second it'll take less time to reach the road. Once on the road, we can go more quickly."

Pluriel looked keenly at Tristal. "Which do you think is the better choice?"

He didn't hesitate. "The second. There are two advantages to it considering we're afraid the Flokav will follow us. First, they won't expect us to take such an open road, and second, they'll probably assume we'd take the faster, more direct route." He glanced back up at Pluriel, hope for approval evident in his eyes. "What do you think?"

"Let me see that map." Tristal handed the parchment over, and Pluriel examined it briefly. "I think you're right, Tristal. We'll cut northwest across the country and join the road about three leagues from the mountains."

It was nearly two hours past midday when they joined up with the Old West Road, the trading route which crossed Militer from Milltam in Gaush all the way to Royaleisia in Staran. It was paved with grey stone, now cracked and mossy from age. This stretch of the Road, from Lazia to Drista, was several hundred years old. Weeds peeked up through cracks in the stone – flowers and grass and dandelions. Surrounding the Road on either side were pastures, but far to the north the peaks of the North Mountains were just visible, stabbing upwards into the clouds. Ahead of them, the Mountains of Fortaer loomed up.

"If you think this a regal spectacle," Ringard murmured to Galdore, who was taking in the view with awe, "go one day and climb to the peak of one of the North Mountains, and gaze southward. From the tip of Mount Royaledh you will see all of Fortaer laid out below you. If your eyesight is keen you can also glimpse the Mountains of Gaush and Fortaer hemming in the lowlands. You will never set eyes on a more wonderful thing."

"If it is more wonderful than this," Galdore answered, "I think I might die if I saw it."

# 6

THE ROAD WAS EMPTY BESIDES THEMSELVES, BUT EVERY now and then they would hear a crashing in the bracken to one side. They grew more and more frustrated as it kept pace with them, but they wanted haste, and as long as the creature gave no trouble they would not waste time to find out what it was. At least they knew it couldn't be Flokav, or they would have been attacked by now.

As night fell they pitched camp, though they had reached the foot of the Pass. The air was still warm, and they sat in the shade to eat their evening meal.

"How far do you think we have to go yet?"

asked Tristal with his mouth full.

"Perhaps twenty-four leagues," replied Ringard. "It will likely take a week to cross Staran."

Tristal began to ask another question, but the crashing started up in the bushes directly behind them. Pluriel sighed and stood up.

"Show yourself!"

A shrill, nasal voice replied, "You got food?"

Galdore raised his eyebrows at Pluriel.

"If you are hungry, we will share what we have."

A stooped old man appeared before them. His long white hair was a matted mess; his clothes hung off his bony frame in tatters, and his face was drawn into a pinched, hungry look.

"What is your name?" asked Pluriel gently.

"My name? My name?" The man looked confused. "Oh, my name! You want my name!"

"I do," answered Pluriel patiently.

"My name..." The man paused and grinned confidingly. "My name... is Gonor."

"Then, Gonor, *hana-gawë*!"

"*Hana, hana, hana-gawë!*" chortled Gonor.

Galdore shot a look at Pluriel. "Raving mad!" he exclaimed under his breath.

Gonor turned to Galdore. "He says I am mad,

mad, mad, raving mad!" He returned his green eyes to Pluriel. "Food, you got food? You said you got food."

"I did," replied Pluriel, and gestured at Tristal. "Give him some food."

Tristal pulled a chunk of bread from the loaf and handed it to the madman, who stuffed the entire piece at once into his mouth. He tried to speak through it, but whatever he was saying was entirely incomprehensible. He swallowed with a gulp, then said, "Kind man he is, kind man with his head so sunny. Gives poor Gonor food, he does, and fills my starving stomach."

"Where are you going to?" Ringard inquired. "Where are you from?"

A faraway look came into Gonor's eyes and when he spoke, it seemed his mind was a little clearer.

"From Gaush I came once, from Gaush of the tall mountains and cold mountain streams, Gaush of bright copper and gems the colour of leaves in spring, Gaush of cold snow and rain. To Evilka I went once, to Evilka of dread towers and blood-filled rivers, Evilka of Flokav and bears and wolves, Evilka of..." The glassy look reappeared in his eyes. "Evilka of the Dark Lord!"

All four men stepped backwards, covering

their ears, for Gonor's voice had risen and become a shriek, a shriek of pure terror and loathing and hatred. Tears filled the lunatic's eyes and he fell to the ground, writhing in the dust and sobbing.

"They took him there," he cried, "they caught him and they took him from his wife and newborn son, they took him to the Towers and they tortured him! They killed his wife and baby son, and they killed Gonor! They killed him, and he's dead, yes, I'm dead. Dead, dead, dead!" His voice rose again. "But he'll kill him, Gonor will kill the Dark Lord, yes, he'll kill him dead, and find his wife and son, and he'll go back to Gaush, Gaush of soft grass and tall trees and mountains." The weeping voice faded into wracking sob.

Sheer pity filled the eyes of Gonor's audience, and Pluriel knelt in front of the old man and tenderly raised him in his arms. The wasted body was a light burden, and Pluriel laid Gonor softly on his own blankets. The fathomless green eyes lit on Pluriel's face.

"They're kind, they're kind to me, they give me food and rest. Gonor hasn't tasted bread or felt soft blankets since he was young, no, not since my wife and son were with me." He trailed off and his eyes closed. Silence descended upon the company.

"There goes our chance of haste," murmured Tristal. "We can't possibly leave him in the wilderness to starve. He is utterly pitiable."

"I wonder why," mused Galdore. "Why did Jalavak think Gonor could help him? Or did he only want to cause more suffering?"

"The latter is my guess," growled Ringard. "Jalavak finds the suffering of the weak and the innocent a delight."

A snore issued from the lips of the madman, and they all turned toward him. A look of peace lay on his emaciated face, but as they looked or closely they could make out wrinkled white scars on his cheeks and forehead, jagged scars that had been closed for decades but never tended as they should. As they gazed at him, he began to talk in his sleep, as though dreaming of something that had passed before.

"I don't know, I don't know, I tell you, I don't know! He never told me!" Gonor thrashed about. "I swear I am speaking the truth!" He stilled, then screamed sharply. "No, no, no! She knows nothing! Don't touch her! Wynna, my love, don't tell him a thing!" His eyes had flown open, although he still slept, and he frantically stared into nothing.

A couple minutes passed in stillness, then his body relaxed and his voice calmed slightly. "Wynna, you didn't tell him about it. Please tell me you didn't betray his trust!" He paused as though he were being answered. "Thank Elamm'. And our son?" The voice rose in fear again. "Wynna, our son? Is Armald safe?" Another pause, and the old man burst into tears, calling on Elamm' and crying out the names of his wife and child in anguish that was dreadful to behold.

# 7

WHEN THE COMPANY AWOKE THE NEXT MORNING, Gonor was up already, capering around and singing nonsense to the sky. He saw Tristal sit up and leapt over to him.

"You are awake, kind man with the sun on his head!" He fingered a lock of Tristal's bright golden hair. "Food, is there more food?"

Tristal yawned and crawled over to his pack. He gave Gonor a piece of bread, and the man sat down and ripped into it ravenously. Pluriel, Ringard, and Galdore joined them and they broke their fast together. Pluriel was restless and continuously glanced over at Gonor as if he were about to ask a question, but seemingly changed his mind at the last moment. Instead he occupied himself with his breakfast.

Gonor sat off by himself whilst they cleared up their belongings. The men kept an eye on him at first to make sure he did not wander off, but Gonor did not seem inclined to go far. They assumed he intended to stay near them, where he would have food and warmth at night.

The Lazia had been fed by melting snow plunging from the mountains, but here, only a little farther north, the mountains were still covered in snow and the air was below freezing point. Shivering, everyone regretted not having brought furs, having forgotten that the mountain air would still be so cold this early in the spring. Gonor, however, seemed oblivious to the bitter temperature and kept well ahead of the others. From time to time he peered back and called some nonsense words. They tramped through snow for hours, pausing only briefly at noon for a quick bite to eat. Just as the sun began to go down, they reached the summit of the Pass. Tristal turned, looked downwards, and gasped.

Ringard laughed. "It does make you afraid of heights, doesn't it!"

Tristal nodded mutely, backing away from the drop-off. Gonor bounded over to investigate, and if Tristal had not thrown out both arms just in time, the old man would have been over the cliff and falling into nothing – the precipice rose many feet high and the ground below was invisible in the gathering dusk.

"Hurry up," Pluriel called back. "If we want to reach the cabin while we can still see, we'll have to leave now."

It had begun to sprinkle freezing rain, and they trudged off, pulling up their hoods. The rain soon increased to a downpour, and little pellets of hail stung where they struck the men's faces. They pushed through the heightening storm, heads down against the wind. Finally the cabin came into sight, and they stumbled up to it and burst into its slight warmth.

The building had been erected for the convenience of traders, but looked as if it had been abandoned for some time. Galdore surveyed the place carefully as they entered, paying special attention to the roof. "Probably leaks," he muttered as his eyes swept over the clapboard. But there was no water dripping down, and they dropped their packs from aching backs.

Hours later, Ringard woke with a start and the feeling that he had heard something. All was pitch black and silent, and after a few minutes he lay down again, thinking he must have been awoken by an unrecalled dream. But he was unsatisfied by the explanation, for he could not shake the idea that he had indeed heard a noise that was out of place. Still, it did not occur again, and after puzzling over it for a while he turned on his side to go back to sleep.

Then he heard it again: a soft squelch just outside the cabin. He at bolt upright, heart thumping, listening very carefully. Then something, or someone, fumbled with the latch of the door. Ringard sprang up, snatching his sword which lay naked beside his pillow, and made his way softly to the door.

The door opened smoothly, silently, and Ringard's arm shot out to catch the arm of a cloaked figure.

"Who are you?" he whispered harshly.

The intruder pulled sharply backward, extricating himself from Ringard's grasp. "Is this not a place where any might stay to rest their limbs?" The voice was low. "But behold!"

A light flickered suddenly in the blackness,

and a bright radiance grew around the figure. Ringard fell back, shielding his eyes, and the same voice, yet inexplicably changed, spoke out of the glow.

"Behold! I am a messenger sent you from Elamm'! You have undertaken this journey on his urging. I am sent to aid you in the accomplishment of this task. For it is difficult night to impossibility, but it is not without hope."

The voice was clearly that of a woman, but pitched slightly differently than woman's wont: it was deeper, or perhaps it was higher: the difference between a low note and a high seemed inconsequential. And the very sound of it was a song, a brilliant music that made Ringard want to sing and laugh and dance. To resist the impulse took an effort which sapped all his strength. He wanted to ask a second time, "Who are you?", but some power prevented him from doing so, and also from falling on his knees, as he felt he ought to do.

"Nay, do not bow before me, for like you I am but a creature," spoke the song again, and Ringard felt that his soul was laid bare and that this being saw somehow his silent desire. "Bow only before Elamm', for in the Book of Laws it is said, "Those who worship one other than Elamm' shall die, for Elamm' reigns supreme over all the earth.'"

With a wrench of his will, Ringard stepped back and said, "Then how shall I honour you, for you seem to me as an angel or a god?"

"You shall not honour me," replied the being, "but treat me as a creature of Elamm' like yourself."

The light dimmed and disappeared. A choking sensation washed over Ringard, and he gulped in mouthfuls of the crisp night air, feeling that it was abnormally sweet and fresh. A sudden dawn burst over the mountain, and the cabin was filled with warm sunlight. Before Ringard stood a figure, cloaked and veiled in immaculate white unsoiled by the dirt floor. Behind Ringard, his four companions stirred and awoke. Ringard turned slowly round to face them, tearing his gaze from the white-robed figure with a hard mental struggle.

"Up early, Ringard?" asked his brother cheerfully.

Ringard shook his head wordlessly and stepped sideways, revealing the figure who had been hidden by his form. And now Gonor did a strange thing. He rose from his blanket and, crossing the cabin to the woman, clutched the sleeves of her robe and began to weep. Still more startling was the woman's reaction. With one hand she slipped off her hood, revealing hair of the brightest gold imaginable, brighter than the hair of Galdore and Tristal, more dazzling than the sun. Then she stooped down from her tall height and put her arms about the little old man.

"Gonor, you have been faithful, faithful where many men would have abandoned honour and spoken. Much you have suffered for your loyalty, but soon now you will be released from your afflictions. Keep strength but a little longer, my friend! You will receive your award before long."

Resisting the urge to sing, Pluriel tore his gaze from the woman and dropped it on his brother. "Who is she?"

The woman looked up; releasing Gonor, she rose. "I am sent by Elamm' to aid you in your undertaking. And – " as Pluriel, Galdore, and Tristal made to kneel, " – I have said already to Ringard that I am no more than a creature of Elamm'. Do not worship me!" The men straightened. "You have heard rightly that the

Sword of the Star is guarded by a dragon, after whom the Swamp is named. Nevarra is old and sly, and her master Jalavak sees far, for he is of the Valintari. You must keep your wits about you from this moment on, for he and she both will endeavour to ensnare you in falsehood."

"And what are we to call you?" whispered Galdore.

The woman fixed the young man with an intense stare, and he instantly coloured and looked down at his feet. "You shall call me Assiel for the present," she replied, "and in time I will give you my true name."

# 8

KYLYN CARRIED A PILE OF DIRTY PLATES INTO THE kitchen and dumped the chicken out the back window. Under Gydi's supervision, the boy had grown healthier and his cheeks were rosy now. He really was too pretty to be a boy, Gydi thought for what must have been the millionth time since Kylyn had arrived a week and a half ago. Again he found himself looking more closely at the boy, and under his stare the roses in Kylyn's cheeks deepened.

"Why do you do that all the time?" His original shyness had dissipated along with his paleness, for Gydi was a very kind man under his stern exterior.

Gydi turned around and guiltily clattered the dishes he had been washing. "No reason," he replied.

"You do it all the time," Kylyn stated positively. "Do you think I'm a thief?"

"Certainly not!" exclaimed Gydi, swinging round again. "I've never missed a thing since you've been here."

"That's good, since I'd like you to remember me kindly when I'm gone – and I think I'll be on my way tomorrow. You said you'd give me enough food to get to Tímil, and from there it's only a short ways to Tarcap, where I should be able to get work, it's such a big place."

Gydi's heart fell into his boots. "How do you even know where you're making to? I thought you said you didn't know and didn't care."

"One of the travellers let me see his map. I saw him looking at it and asked if I might."

His disappointment at the thought of Kylyn leaving fled and he glared at the kid. "If I've told you once not to bother the guests, I've told you a hundred times, Kylyn! You're not to go pestering them, it's not good for business!"

"I wasn't pestering!" protested Kylyn, turning an angry red. "I waited till he'd finished and laid it down and was eating his meal and *then* I asked!"

"Well, what's done is done," observed Gydi gloomily as he returned to his dishes, "but don't do it again."

"I won't, but you won't have to worry about that much longer. I'm leaving tomorrow after breakfast."

Gydi suddenly remembered how the argument had started and his heart sank again. A pity he'd never married; he'd have kids of his own. But it was no use trying to convince Kylyn to stay longer. He knew from ten days of trying to manage him how stubborn he was.

"Are you sure you've got enough food?" he asked as Kylyn stood on the step the next morning, apparently reluctant to leave. "I sure wouldn't want you going hungry."

"Oh yes, plenty. I don't eat much," Kylyn declared, patting the package of *marcin*, long-lasting travelling bread, that sat at his feet.

Gydi snorted. "Not much, no. Just enough for two of your size."

A little smile curved Kylyn's upper lip. "Don't worry about me. I'll be fine."

"I will worry," Gydi muttered. "And I'll miss you, at that."

"I'll miss you too," returned Kylyn. "You've

been so kind, and I'll never forget you." In the momentary silence that followed, he rubbed his chapped lips together. "You know what, Gydi? I'll tell you a secret, if you swear you won't get mad at me."

Gydi grinned. "A secret... as in, you're a girl, not a boy. And maybe even the runaway servant girl they were asking about last week."

The ready blush splashed onto Kylyn's face. "Just so. And my name's Eloderaẏ."

Gydi stepped forward and gave the kid a hug. "Good boy – good girl, I mean."

Kylyn – Eloderaẏ – smiled and returned his hug. But as she tried to pull free, he caught her hand with one of his and shoved the other into his apron pocket. Into her protesting hand he poured a small clinking shower of coins.

"Like I said, don't want you starving to death," he muttered, and quickly turned back into the inn.

"*Sariënh, ledh samach ne!*"[1] called Eloderaẏ after him, and set off down the road. On the outskirts of the town, she stopped and opened her hand. It was filled with coins, not only copper pennies, but also a silver denhl, worth fifty pennies! And her pack was filled with food, and someone had shown her affection for the first time within

[1] "Goodbye and thank you!"

memory.

Eloderaý felt absolutely rich.

"There! Staran!" Ringard emphasised his words with a wide sweeping gesture of his arm. His eyes shone at the sight of his beloved homeland, which he had not seen in several years. Pluriel, too, looked almost overcome with joy. Galdore and Tristal, watching the other pair of brothers, could see why they so loved this land. From where they stood, still a ways up the mountain, they could see the lush greenness of the grass and trees and the bright flowers dotting the ground at intervals. The sun, which was beginning to set, cast a pinkish glow over the scene. The soft beauty of the scene smote closer to their hearts than the splendour of the mountains.

North to Tarcap they went now, through the meadows that sprang to new life almost before their eyes. Spring came in earnest to Staran. Ahead of them went Assiel, Gonor clinging to her hand.

"Now Pluriel," said Galdore, "do you agree with Tristal and me that this woman is the one who rescued us from the Flokav?"

Pluriel nodded.

"And now will you tell us your theory about her?"

"No."

Galdore pursed his lips and turned away. He felt as though he should know what Pluriel and Ringard were thinking, but he couldn't put his thoughts in order regarding it. Why did they keep it such a secret?

King Leftar sat hunched over a table with his face dropped into his hands. He ignored all who came begging hi to eat or drink, for he had taken neither meat nor wine, neither moved from his position nor spoken, for an entire day. His wife sat across the table from him, saying nothing, but watching her husband with an unwavering stare. Knowing him well, the Queen moved not even when tears began to squeeze through his fingers.

At last the King moved. He looked up at Lalethiel and smiled, but his eyes were wet with tears, and grief stared out of them.

"I think this is the end, my love."

A silent question was in the Queen's eyes

that did not drop.

"Fortaer will attack Jalavak."

Lalethiel showed no sign of shock or fear. "And do you go with the men?"

"I am the King. I do not send my people to meet alone what I will not meet."

"Then I go also. I would not leave you. What you face, I will face. If you fall, I will fall at your side." She rose a rustle of skirts. "I will summon our son."

Leftar nodded. Queen Lalethiel went slowly from the room, her husband's gaze following her. Her stature was decidedly that of a queen: tall and straight and slender, and the beauty of girlhood had never diminished in her face. But now for the first time her back was bowed and she walked with a slight stoop that had not been there ten minutes earlier. And the stoop told of all the burden of dread and sorrow that she would not show to her husband.

A few minutes passed before Prince Kedýran entered the chamber, a tall handsome youth of eighteen summers. His cheeks were bronzed from an outdoor life, and his reddish-brown hair fell in a characteristic mess just past his shoulders. Upon seeing his father's distress he immediately rounded the table to kneel at his side.

"What is going on, *dẃnhl*?"

Leftar leaned his head on his son's shoulder. "Begin the muster of the army, *sularh amh*. We ride for Evilka three dawns from now."

# 9

TRISTAL AND GALDORE FELT LOST AS THEY TURNED their heads from side to side, gaping at the buildings. They were much different from the houses in Fortaer: marble instead of clay bricks, carven stone instead of logs. It was quite disconcerting for them, and Tristal quite forgot to keep a firm hold on Gonor, who continuously tried to escape in search of Assiel, who had disappeared as soon as they'd entered Tarcap. Suddenly he realised and choked.

"Gonor's gone!"

His brother wheeled and stared at him. "You let him go in the middle of Tarcap? Tristal, there are fifteen hundred people in this city. How are we supposed to find him?"

"I didn't mean to, obviously," replied Tristal sulkily, and looked ahead down the road with a stern look on his face.

Pluriel's face went blank as he concealed his irritation. "We'll just have to search for him, then. We'll spread out, and meet in the town square in two hours' time. All right?"

Galdore and Ringard nodded in agreement and left immediately in opposite directions. Tristal was about to go as well but Pluriel caught his arm. Tristal turned to face him, and Pluriel couldn't help smiling; the young man clearly expected a reproach. "Don't worry, Tristal, we'll find him again. He can't have gotten far." Tristal's expression clearly a tiny bit. "But do pay more attention next time. Who knows what he might get into all alone."

Tristal nodded and pulled away hastily, and they separated.

Tristal took a narrow way that led eastward. There were few people in the street but the roadway was so tight that it seemed crowded. He pushed his way impatiently past everyone in his path, eager to be the one who found Gonor and regain Pluriel's trust. So fervent was he that he failed to notice as the road took him deeper and deeper into the slummier regions of Tarcap, and the overhanging buildings cast a dark shadow over the streetway below. Suddenly he gave a shiver and finally realised how far he must have come. He wondered what time it was and thought maybe he should begin heading back to the centre of town, for he didn't even know where the square was.

Disappointed he would probably not find Gonor after all, he cast one more look around before turning back. Shadows lurked everywhere and Tristal perceived for the first time how poor his surroundings were. Refuse was piled along the walls of the close-set houses and cast a smell all through the street. Wrinkling his nose, he began to pick his way along; bereft of his mission, he noticed everything that was disgusting about the neighbourhood.

As a boy he had always imagined that Staran was completely different from Fortaer – that there was no poverty, that everything was bright and clean and merry. Now that he thought about it, he saw he'd unconsciously equated the

Startern with the Elves of the old tales, but that was obviously the wrong idea. For sure the Startern were wise and tall and beautiful, and long-lived, but they were not actually immortal, and they were quite as capable of evil and cruelty as any man, whereas the Elves in the epics never served an enemy of Elamm'.

He was pondering these reflections when he became aware that he was no longer alone. A man walked silently at his side. Out of the corner of his eye Tristal took in his appearance: he was medium height, not much taller than Tristal himself; his green tunic and brown cloak were well-kept and out-of-place with their surroundings. His hair was golden; his eyes were bright blue, but they contained a hard glint to which Tristal developed an immediate aversion. It gave an otherwise pleasing countenance an unattractive look.

"*Hana-gawĕ*," said the stranger as he observed Tristal's furtive examination.

Tristal replied in like manner, but returned his eyes to the road ahead, trying to convey that he had no interest in a conversation. The stranger must have caught the hint, but it did not deter him. "So, what is a young gentlemen like yourself doing here?"

"Nothing," answered Tristal, annoyed.

"Surely you don't walk here for pleasure?"

"And why should I not?" Tristal quickened his pace. The other man quickened his own to keep up.

"This isn't the safest place for a lone man who looks as well-off as you do. I'm sure you've noticed."

Finally Tristal turned to face his companion. "You look wealthier than I do – and you're alone."

The stranger smiled. "I'm known in these parts, my young friend."

Tristal bristled at the patronising epithet and lost his temper. "Then why don't you go visit your fine friends and leave me alone, for pity's sake!"

The man raised his eyebrows with an affronted air. "Well, if you feel that way about it!"

He fell back a couple steps, and if Tristal had not increased his pace immediately without looking back, he would have seen his erstwhile companion signalling to someone just within a doorway. The second person in turn signalled behind him and five tall dark figures slipped out. They crept up behind Tristal, then the first clapped his hand over the young man's mouth and yanked him backwards.

"WhanMilter'shapnin!" Tristal exclaimed through the hand.

"This, my young friend, is what happens to people who displease me." The man in the green tunic chuckled and folded his arms, watching the struggle with amusement.

Tristal managed to twist around to see who was holding him. The face was sunburnt to a crispy near-black except for the nose, which was pale. The eyes were red; each ear had one red dot on the lobe.

"Flokav?" he tried to exclaim, but the restraining hand prevented him.

"Let him go now, Badgut." The Floka obeyed. "Let's be polite," continued the man. "I'll introduce myself. My name is Eparne, and yes, before you ask, I am Leftar's nephew, curse him. You need not introduce yourself. I know your name, Tristal, and I know your brother's name, and Ringard's name, and Pluriel's name. I just need the name of your other companion, and once you give it to me you can go back and find Galdore and Ringard and Pluriel."

"Our other companion?" said Tristal, playing for time.

"Oh, don't act dumb." Eparne, governor of Forran, rolled his eyes. "I know very well that you were joined by another. The name of that person is extremely important to me." He advanced on Tristal, bent his face very close to the boy's, and spoke slowly and deliberately. "What is the name of your fifth companion?"

Tristal thought quickly. Clearly, Eparne didn't know about Gonor; he must think Assiel was the only addition to their group.

"Tell me now," growled Eparne.

"Gonor," answered Tristal, perfectly truthfully, for Eparne had asked the name of the fifth, who was technically Gonor.

Eparne jumped back, clearly startled by an answer he did not expect. Then he narrowed his blue eyes at his prisoner. "You're lying to me – and those who lie to me regret it."

"I'm not lying. The fifth member of our company joined us two, three days ago just before we crossed the Matren Pass. His name is Gonor and he's mad."

Eparne nodded to the Flokav again and Badgut returned his grip to Tristal's arms.

"Once I'm finished with you, you'll wish you'd told me the truth, you asinine imbecile," sneered Eparne.

Galdore had headed north almost without think-ing consciously about his choice, something inside him suggesting that Gonor's instinct would be to go farther from Evilka. Sure enough, he came upon him within an hour, sitting in the gutter and singing nonsense. Galdore, approach-ing from down the street, could both see and hear him, and a couple passers-by tossed him a penny with a laugh.

Galdore jogged the last stretch to the madman, who smiled up at him beatifically.

"There you are, there you are. I wondered where you all wen' off to and left me all alone here. But where's my friend with the hair so sunny?"

"He's looking for you elsewhere. Come, we've got to go find him."

The idea of finding Tristal motivated Gonor and they managed to make quite a good speed. However, Galdore had to stop several times to ask the way to the square, and it was a few minutes past the two hours when the two came hurrying up to Ringard, who stood alone in the centre of the square.

Ringard looked decidedly relieved when he spotted them, but less so when he glanced around the square again and saw neither Pluriel nor Tristal. "They should be here by now," he fretted. He was nervous, and Gonor saw it.

"He'll come soon, your night-haired brother."

Ringard managed a brief smile, but Gonor's face fell.

"Your sunny-headed brother," he said to Galdore. "He's not coming. He's lost. He's gone. Gone like I was. Lost and hurting and alone."

Galdore's eyes went dark with fear and Ringard shook Gonor's shoulder. "No nonsense, Gonor. That's silly talk."

"Not silly talk. Gonor knows. I know. Lost in the city. Enemies have him; they'll hurt him."

"Enough!" barked Ringard, then he looked up to see Pluriel hurrying across the square. "Pluriel! Have you seen Tristal?"

"Not since we parted back there." Pluriel's voice trailed off. "No one's seen him?"

"He's lost," muttered Gonor, and this time Ringard did not rebuke him. Galdore stared at the madman and his lips moved wordlessly, reliving a long-forgotten memory. "Lost and hurting and alone," Gonor murmured apologetically, and dropped his eyes from Galdore's stare.

"Sometimes madmen see clearest of all," Pluriel said quietly. He set his hand on Galdore's shoulder, and he started.

"Never do that again!" he cried.

"Galdore!" Pluriel shook him a little. "Wake up."

Galdore shuddered and came out of his trance. "I'm sorry," he whispered. "When he was a kid Tristal got lost and I couldn't find him for so long. So long..."

"He's fine, Galdore," Ringard said quickly as Galdore lost focus again. *Go look for him,* he mouthed to his brother. "Tell me about it, Galdore."

"He was five. *Dwnhl* was away with business, *alahs* was sick in bed. He ran away. I looked for hours, right up to the palace at the last, and there he was playing on the steps with a lady who was crying. She was beautiful, mournful and beautiful." Galdore's eyes snapped back into focus. "Ringard, where's Tristal?"

"Are you all right?"

"I'm fine. Where's Tristal? I have to find him!"

"Wait!" cried Ringard, but Galdore had taken off as fast as he could run, and Gonor was clinging to Ringard's arm.

# 10

SHE HAD NO IDEA WHERE TO GO.

Eloderaẏ turned repeatedly in circles, trying to figure out which way was south. At last she selected one road and started down it. She soon found that it merely led her deeper into Tarcap and, looking up at the morning sun, discovered that she was going east rather than south. Frustrated, she took a turn to her right. This street moved into a dank region of the city and Eloderaẏ recoiled from the reeking smells.

It was only when she was feeling hopelessly lost and confused that she spotted a man coming down the street towards her. Encouraged by his almost-respectable appearance in the midst of the slum, she hurried up to him.

"Pardon me, sir, but could you tell me the way to the southern edge of the city?"

The man grinned at her as his green eyes raked over her head to toe, taking in the boy's clothes she still wore, and her hair, which she had clumsily cut with a knife.

"Keep on the way yeh're going, son; yeh'll come ter it soon enow. This street leads righ' through t' th'edge o' town."

"Thank you very much!"

Eloderaý hurried on past the man, but couldn't resist sneaking a look behind her to make sure he wasn't following. He disappeared around a corner, and she went on in haste. Then she heard a cry of pain.

She drew up short, recognising the distressingly familiar sound. Instinctively she contorted her arm to scratch her back where a healed welt suddenly itched.

There was another cry, and this time she pinpointed the house from which it came. Perfectly aware that she was probably about to get into a good deal of trouble, she approached the building warily. The sound of the screams led her to the back of the house, squeezing between it and its close-set neighbour to find her way into the squashed, foul back alley.

Up the back wall crawled a thick covering of ivy as though it had been set there for her alone. She smiled a little as she grasped the thick cord-like branches and pulled herself up a few feet. With the strength she had gained under Gydi's care, it was short work to reach the height of the second-storey window. Cautiously she peered around the windowframe, and then drew back so sharply that she nearly lost her grip.

A young man lay face down on the floor, back bloodied by the whip raised by a man who faced towards Eloderaý's window. As Eloderaý flattened herself against the wall, praying she had not been seen, the older man snarled and snapped the whip in the air.

"Are you going to tell me yet, fool?"

"I told you the first time," gasped the other.

"You lied!"

"I... did not."

The whip cracked, and the young man drew in a sobbing breath.

"I... did... not..." he repeated.

The man with the whip tremulously sucked in air as though holding his temper in check. "You started out with four. You were joined by a fifth. A woman."

"A man!" returned the young man, and the temper wrested free, the whip cracking cruelly three times. Then the older man seemed to withdraw as his voice distanced itself from the window.

"I'll return in an hour. Use that time to make a wise decision."

A door slammed, and, left alone, the young man began to sob softly. Eloderaÿ's heart swelled with pity, and she made a swift decision. She flung one leg over the windowsill and pulled her whole body after it. The boy's head flew up and he stared at her in shock.

"Shush," she cautioned before he could speak. "We must make haste."

"How in Militer did you find me?" he asked.

"Questions later," she replied. She unwrapped her bundle and handed her water bottle to him; he drank avidly. "Let me have that back." He passed it to her, and she poured some out onto the apron that had wrapped her bundle. She gently dabbed at the bleeding welts, he wincing each time the cold wet cloth touched his back.

"All right, now get up and put this on – and hurry." She passed him his shirt and busied herself repacking everything into the damp aprons. When she turned back to him, he was standing, cringing as the fabric caught at his sores.

"Are you okay?" she asked.

"Yes," he ground out through clenched teeth. "I'll be fine. Just help me through the window."

"You'll have to climb down the ivy..." She glanced anxiously at his face.

"So?"

Either he was ill-natured, or more likely it stung that she had seen him cry. Eloderaý bit off a sharp comeback and helped him as he had asked. She stood above him as he made his way slowly down, each new handhold clutched like a lifeline. Once he reached the ground he spread-eagled against the wall and she climbed down after him.

"We can't go openly down the street," she whispered. "We'd be seen."

"You have a better way?"

She stepped away from the wall to reconnoitre, but he caught her arm and yanked her back against the house beside him.

"Are you *crazy*?"

She flushed. "I just wanted to... oh, nothing. Our only choice is down the alley."

"Okay then!" He gave her a *Come on!* look and

led the way through the alley. They skirted innumerable rotting heaps of who knew what, and more than once they narrowly missed being doused by some kind of liquid tossed from an upper window. Finally they reached the end of the houses and dropped wearily onto a patch of grass so tired from its hopeless struggle for survival that it was little relief from the pavement. But it was an end to the alley.

"Now that that's over," the boy said, "we take a rest. A long rest. Maybe a very long rest." He rolled onto his front and buried his face in the grass with a moan of pleasure. "Now tell me who you are and how you found me and things like that."

Eloderaẏ laughed slightly. "Well, my name is Eloderaẏ, I'm sixteen, and I come from Tralaga. I got lost in the slum and happened to hear you crying out, so I thought I should do something."

"Why's that?" he asked probingly, giving her a once-over. "Why should you care?"

She dropped her gaze and plucked two strands of grass from the dirt, knotting them together. "No one should be left to such a punishment."

"So you decided to risk yourself to rescue me."

"Yeah."

She said no more, and he was silent too, staring at her. Finally he said, "And I'm Tristal. Twenty-one. From Fortaer."

Eloderaý looked up in relief at the change in subject. "So why was he beating you?"

Tristal's face closed off. "None of your business."

"I answered your question about my own why."

"As vaguely as you could."

She made a snap decision, ignoring the risk of telling a stranger she was a runaway. "My real why for your why."

He narrowed his eyes at her. Then spoke. "Nope."

She accepted his refusal – or pretended to – and passed him a piece of bread from her pack. "You're probably starving."

Tristal thanked her and ripped into it.

"I assume," he said as he finished eating, "that since you are a girl but wearing male clothes, you have absconded from somewhere."

"None of your business," she echoed him.

"Of course," he said, and laughed.

"Does your back still hurt?"

"I'll be all right."

"Do you want to try and find your companions?"

Tristal sat up. "Yeah... but I have no idea where they are and I don't want to come across Eparne again."

"True," she replied, but Tristal's attention was suddenly focussed behind her.

"Assiel!"

Eloderaý turned around, and all at once she was paralysed on the ground as Tristal leapt up. And then the woman spoke. Eloderaý's tongue came unhinged and without meaning to, she began to sing.

*Our princess dear went off one day;*
*Now where she is no man can say.*
*To eradicate evil was her intent:*
*To Evilka Murkena went.*

She began the second stanza when she suddenly became conscious of what she was doing and fell silent, abashed. Tristal was smiling at her as though he knew something she didn't, and the woman's unearthly expression was unfathomable. Then she repeated what she had said when Eloderaý had started to sing.

"Come, my children; I will take you to your friends."

# 11

THIS TIME NOT SPLITTING UP, PLURIEL, RINGARD, AND Galdore wandered through the streets with Gonor in tow, searching everywhere for Tristal. Galdore didn't even try to hide his despair; he loved his brother more than he ever would have admitted.

"Why, it's the Frosindalion!"

Pluriel and Ringard swung around at the sound of their father's name, and Ringard caught the speaker in an embrace.

"Elwyn!"

"Ringard, I haven't seen you or your brother for a year! What brings you to Tarcap?"

"We cannot speak of it publicly," replied Pluriel, elbowing his brother aside and embracing Elwyn himself. "How are you, cousin?"

"I'm well in body, but a shadow grows in my mind as the power of Jalavak waxes." Elwyn's smile faded; then he looked over at Galdore and Gonor. "Introduce us?"

Ringard obliged.

Galdore stepped forward a tad shyly and stretched out his hand. The two men grasped each other's wrists in the common manner of greeting, and inclined their heads slightly. Then Elwyn looked back at his cousins.

"We can speak in private at the edge of the city."

After they had explained their quest to Elwyn, the Startern lord sat deep in thought.

"As I said before, Jalavak's power waxes, ever more as the year progresses. Kanethon and I have spoken much of this. I think you must make all possible haste if you are to be in time."

Pluriel nodded. "I've been thinking the same thing myself, that we must hurry. I think we can make Duskmoor Keep in about five days now. After that... well, we'll see."

"And what do you plan to do with the Sword? Do you have any plan?"

"We thought to deliver it to King Kanethon to use as he sees fit..."

"I have news that you will not yet have heard, I think," said Elwyn as Ringard trailed off lamely. "King Leftar sent a message to Kanethon by Fortaer's fastest post runners. It arrived early today; the runners made record time. The Fortaerim are to ride on Evilka itself in two days' time." Three gasped simultaneously, but Gonor nodded sagely. "Leftar wanted to know if Kanethon could send any warriors."

"And?" queried Galdore breathlessly.

"Our King is sending his entire army."

Galdore released an excited sigh.

"I can hardly say I'm surprised," said Ringard. "Kanethon never shirked a duty or refused a friend in his life."

"That is so, and the muster of Staran's army began this noon. That, in fact, is the reason I am in Tarcap, for I rode in haste to gather Tarcap's men."

All of a sudden, Galdore cried out joyfully. "Tristal!" He leapt up and ran to embrace his brother, who gave a yelp of pain and pulled away. Galdore's look of joy was relieved by one of fright. "You're hurt?"

"Yes, but as long as you don't touch my back

I'm all right. Assiel's back, and I've brought a new friend." He pulled Eloderaý forward from where she lingered timidly behind him. "Actually, Eloderaý is the one who rescued me."

"Rescued you? Tristal, what's been going on?" Pluriel's tone was upset.

"Thank you," Galdore said softly to Eloderaý.

Tristal closed his eyes, then opened them, and they could see his fury. "The King's own nephew."

For the first time in days Ringard thought of that rumour he'd heard at the Silver Spear. "Eparne?"

Tristal nodded exhaustedly. "He tried to get me to tell him who Assiel was but I refused."

Gonor walked up to Tristal and gently put his arms around him. "Kind Tristal," he murmured, using the young man's name for the first time. "Gonor knows, he knows what Tristal feels. Friends who betrays, Gonor knows that. Enemies who hurts, Gonor knows that too." The cracked voice was unbearably sad. "But you, Tristal," he said softly, "you have your brother still. I lost my family, but yours is left to you. Thank Elamm' for his blessings."

They had said farewell to Lord Elwyn and were a league from Tarcap when Assiel spoke for the first time since she'd rejoined them. They were taking a rest after the noon meal, the men reclining on the ground, Gonor sleeping, Assiel standing with her back to them.

"What exactly is the Sword of the Star?" asked Eloderaý, to whom they had explained matters after Pluriel had grilled her and finally pronounced her safe to join their company.

"According to legend," replied Pluriel, "the Valintara Royaleisia used it in a heavenly war in the first ages of the universe. It was stolen by Jalavak because it is said that it is the sole weapon that might defeat him."

"And why is that?" Eloderaý questioned curiously.

Assiel turned around. "With the Sword of the Star Royaleisia threw Afalin out of the heavens, for he had turned to evil. Royaleisia struck him, with intent only to wound. The blood which he left on the sword blended with the blade. Now Jalavak, for so Afalin is called by the men of Militer, shall not die until that blood mingles again with that which runs in his veins now. No other blade may leave a lasting mark on his flesh."

"It is said, too, that it is not by the hand of

man that he shall fall," observed Ringard.

"That is the truth, for Afalin was a Valintara, and although, because he has killed, his place among the Valintari is surrendered, he still may be killed only by a Valintara."

Tristal sighed. "Then our object is hopeless."

"Why should it be so?"

The sound of Assiel's voice had a way of dispelling any feelings of despair or doubt. "I do not know," he said softly.

She placed her hand on his shoulder and lifted his chin, gazing straight into his eyes. "Never say that *anything* is hopeless, Tristal, until it has irreparably failed. And always remember that Elamm' may perform any action, though it may seem impossible to you."

The depth of Assiel's eyes mesmerized Tristal. They were grey, her eyes: a deep grey like no other eyes he'd ever seen before, a colour akin to that of the sky before a thunderstorm.

"I will remember," he whispered.

# 12

IT WAS A RESTLESS ARMY THAT STOOD READY AT THE break of that dreary dawn. The men of Fortaer would follow their king to the death if he asked it, but that did not mean they must look forward to it. Many had left wives and young children when the King's call came. Not one man that day expected to see his family again.

They brightened a little at the sight of King Leftar. They even roused a weak cheer. The King's eyes surveyed his army, perceiving their fears. Then he began to speak.

"I would let fear dishearten me also, but it would do not good for Militer. Who among you cares for your world, for your land, for your loved ones so that you would fight for the things you hold dear? Or are you all too afraid? If any of you here cares for anything, come with us! And if you are too frightened, then go home and cower there, awaiting the last conquest of our land by the Dark Lord!"

Ashamed, the men muttered amongst themselves. Finally, one man, the leader of the Lazian men, stepped forward.

"Lazia apologises to you for our fear, my lord King. Forgive us. We would follow you anywhere."

An assenting cheer rippled through the army. The captain was about to rejoin his company, but the King caught him by the shoulder. "Thank you," he whispered, then grasped both his wrists in salute.

A very muddy Pluriel struggled at the head of his company, all similarly slimy and dirtied: after Pluriel came Tristal holding Gonor's hand, then Ringard, and Galdore assisting Eloderaý when she stumbled in the murky swamp water, and finally Assiel at the end of the untidy line.

Somehow Assiel's white robes were as immaculately white as an untouched snowfall, though she had made no attempt to save them.

Ahead they could see their goal, Duskmoor Keep, a towering mass of black stone; what exactly the material was, no one knew. Somehow the Keep stood in the middle of the Swamp; there was no solid ground beneath it yet there it had stood for thousands of years. Perhaps it was Jalavak's sorcery that had placed and kept it there; that was the tale of Startern peasants of the nearby area, anywhere. But no one knew for certain what was the mystery of Duskmoor Keep.

At long last they reached the centre of the swamp. A firm path of dried mud let up to the gates. These were closed, but carved upon them was an inscription which Pluriel read aloud. The words told of a password which alone would open the doors, a secret word of Jalavak's. The company exchanged despairing looks, with the exception of Assiel, who remained aloof.

"Then as Tristal thought, this has all been for nothing," began Eloderaý wearily, but was instantly stilled by a glance from Assiel. It wasn't angry, but it made her feel guilty nonetheless.

"We'll just have to camp here tonight," decided Pluriel. "The morning will be a better time to decide what to do."

Miserably they set out their blankets on the unyielding ground and lay down, thinking that little sleep would they get that night. Gonor alone slept the deep sleep of which he seemed capable wherever he lay. The others tossed and turned.

Presently Gonor began to mutter in his sleep. He often did this and his friends merely ignored it now, but soon his ravings had risen to such a pitch that it was no longer possible to tune them out. Sighing in exasperation, all the others sat up as one. It was no use even to try to rest.

"You've destroyed everything that's dear to me; there's nothing anymore that can make me tell you. Hurt me all you like; I no longer feel the pain." The words became scrambled, more like his waking chatter. "Pain of the mind, of the mind, oh no, that cannot hurt me either. We're dead, our heart is dead, our mind is dead, our body is dead. You have no power over us any more, no, you have no power over me." Now all that could be distinguished were random words and bits of sentences. "I swear it... Wynna... the corn is peeping up now... come here, Wynna, quick... I said no and I... I'll never tell a soul... here in a minute, love... hurt her... is dead... I swear it...

don't know anything... don't touch that, Armald... did he mean... *arkghant*..."

There was a creaking noise and all attention flew from Gonor to the gates of the Keep. They were opening slowly, their occasional protest shrieking through the silent night.

"Why can't it be quiet?" was Tristal's first reaction. "The noise'll wake everything in the castle!"

"Where did Gonor hear that word?" Ringard asked of no one in particular.

With a concluding squeak of epic volume, the gates stood wide open. One by one they slipped into the darkness, Assiel entering last after picking up Gonor. Every sound they made was magnified by the echo; the place seemed deserted.

"Maybe there's no dragon after all," said Eloderaý aloud, hopefully but unthinkingly. Galdore clapped a horrified hand over her mouth from behind as her words sang piercingly through the open hall. For a moment she considered apologising, but concluded that she'd caused enough disturbance for the moment – and in any case, Galdore's hand covered her mouth so tightly that she couldn't have spoken even if she'd decided otherwise.

"Not such a good idea," was all the rebuke she received, but Ringard's gentle reprimand only made her feel worse.

Galdore released her but kept her close to him with a restraining hand on her shoulder. Pluriel fumbled his way over to her and took her hand, closing her fingers over the hilt of a sword. Then he leaned near her to whisper in her ear.

"Listen."

Thumping came from somewhere in the dark, fast approaching. There was a ringing as they drew their swords. All of a sudden an unearthly light surged through the hall, revealing ten husky figures which stood at the foot of a staircase some yards ahead. Taking in their appearance, both Tristal and Eloderaý retched. Galdore's face took on a greenish hue. The only change apparent in Ringard and Pluriel was a touch of fear in their dark eyes, but they made no sound. The figures were those of humankind, but the head of each was that of a large bear.

The gates grated and groaned behind them, coming to with a crash. Even had they contemplated flight, it was no longer an option.

The charge of the first three bear-men was met by the swords of Ringard, Galdore, and Pluriel. The bears wrenched themselves off the impaling blades and, enraged, made another attack, this time reinforced by the rest of their number. They drew their own swords, coloured red, Jalavak's colour. Tristal joined his brother and friends and covered himself with glory by being the first to actually kill one. Seven more fell, two each to the swords of Galdore and Pluriel, and three to that of Ringard.

Only two bears remained. The first of them was the largest of all, and it was wounded and mad. To hold it in any manner of check took the strength of all four men, and the second bear was free to do as it pleased.

It pleased to attack Eloderaý.

The girl paled but held her ground. It was her fault the bear-men were here; it was her duty to help her friends kill them. She thought back to Mistress Stellatin for the briefest of seconds, wondering if she should have stayed despite the abuse. Then she steeled herself and met the bear's gaze.

As it brought down its sword to cleave her in two, she raised her own and met the blow. The shock of the meeting ran up her blade, through the hilt, and into her hand and arm. She almost lost her grip, but recovered just in time to block another thrust. She flailed her sword about, trusting to luck that it would go where it needed to be. Then she made an intentional move. The bear's neck was unprotected. She might well be killed in the doing of it, but...

She risked it.

Her sword went straight through the bear's neck. It capered about in agony, but she held the weapon as steady as she could. Then, without warning, the bear's arm jerked upwards in its deathdance, and the blade which it still clutched sliced half an inch through Eloderay's left arm.

She let go her sword with a cry and crumpled to the floor, simultaneously with the bear. Galdore sprang forward, the other bear also dead, and caught her just before her head struck the stone flags. She lay faint in his arms, and the others clustered around.

With his free hand Galdore unsheathed a small knife and very gently cut off the blood-soaked sleeve of Eloderay's tunic. The cut was bleeding a good deal, and it looked disgusting.

"Do any of you know anything about medicine?" he asked the others desperately.

Gonor stepped forward.

"No, not you, Gonor," Tristal told him, pulling the old man away. "They need a healer."

"I am a healer," Gonor answered, his eyes

confidently meeting Tristal's.

Then he turned back to Galdore, who stared at Gonor for a few moments. Not once did the madman break his gaze, or even blink. Finally Galdore nodded. Gonor knelt down and gently raised Eloderay's bleeding arm.

"It's not very bad," he said after a while. "But I'll need some herbs to wash it with, and then a cloth to bind it up."

"I'll tear a strip off my tunic for you," offered Galdore at once.

"No, it has to be clean," Gonor answered, giving Galdore's tunic a scathing glance.

Assiel bent down and took up the hem of her unsoiled robe. With a quick twitch of the knife in her hand, she ripped off a long piece four inches in width, and gave it to Gonor.

"What herbs do you need?" she asked him.

"Stem of heartflower, leaf of pipeweed," he replied automatically.

"But where are we going to get them?" questioned Ringard. "Not in the middle of the Nevarra Swamp, for sure."

Tristal sniffed a little. "I've got a couple heartflowers. I remembered how you wanted them, Ringard, when Galdore was bitten by the silisik, so when I noticed some I picked them."

He dug in his pack and drew out two small wilted flowers. The blooms themselves were delicate, shaped nearly like hearts, crisscrossed with tiny golden veins.

"How many do you need?"

"Just one will do."

"I knew it was a good idea to pick them," Tristal said, passing Gonor one and carefully packing away the other.

"But the pipeweed!" Gonor interrupted irritably.

"Pipeweed..." said Pluriel with a groan. "I don't suppose you have any of that, Tristal?"

Just then Eloderaẏ's eyes flicked open. "My arm aches," she complained at once. Then, "What on earth were those things?"

"Jogens," Pluriel answered her laconically. "Do you have any pipeweed by some chance?"

"Why? Do you smoke?"

Pluriel grimaced. "Of course not."

"Actually, I do have some, now I come to think of it," said Eloderaẏ. "I picked some out of a field on my way from Kefield to Carda. I know I shouldn't have, but it was only a few leaves. I thought I might like to have some to remember Tralaga by – though I don't know why I wanted to remember my life there. I've always liked the smell of a pipe."

"Stop talking and give it me!" growled Gonor.

"Why?"

Galdore cleared his throat and her eyes flipped up to him.

"Oh yes," she said vaguely. "I was meaning to ask you why you were holding me."

Galdore flushed; Tristal snorted.

"Your arm is cut," explained Pluriel. "The pipeweed is to wash the wound."

Immediately Eloderaý craned to see her arm, and gagged.

"That's a lotta blood," she muttered.

Galdore turned her face away. "No need to look at that."

"The pipeweed's in my pack if you must have some," she said sulkily. "Try not to use it all, please."

Tristal quickly found the weed and gave it to Gonor. He tore up the herbs and mixed them with a little water, creating a sort of mush. This he smeared over the wound, then took Assiel's bandage and wrapped it tightly around the arm. Eloderaý remained alert throughout the entire procedure, but let out no more than an anguished squeak from time to time, clutching at Galdore with her good hand.

# 13

Gonor was cleaning up from the operation when a padding noise above them became audible. Stepping softly down the stairs came the dragon, its body twenty feet long, its wingspan fifty wide. It crawled near to them, then stopped but a couple yards away. For a while it simply stared at them. Then it opened its mouth.

"You ought to be dead."

The dragon's voice was husky and mesmerising, each word spoken very deliberately. Whilst it spoke, the men and Eloderaý could not rip their eyes from its own.

"You ought to be dead, but I suppose you

killed all my guards before they could kill you. That was not a nice thing to do, you know. They were my friends as well as my guards. You must be quite clever to have killed ten jogens."

No one answered.

"I shall introduce myself. My name is Nevarra, and I am the right hand of Jalavak. Now you must tell me your names."

Still no one answered the dragon.

Nevarra slithered towards Tristal and her eyes drove into his like swords.

"You, boy. What is your name?"

"Tristal." He spoke against his will – but what was his will, after all? Did free will even exist? Did Elamm' exist... or was he as unreal as free will? Was there only one will in Militer, that of Jalavak and, through him, Nevarra? Was there anything besides this quiet command within his mind that forced him to answer? Tristal quivered – but no, the will had not told him he may quiver. He stood unmoving. He tried to think – but no, the will had not told him he may think. He was dead to all but the dragon's eyes.

Nevarra moved on to Galdore and simply gazed at him. He gave his name after the briefest of pauses. The same happened to all the men, and Eloderaÿ. Their eyes now involuntarily followed the serpentine movements whether the dragon was speaking or no.

Then Nevarra came to Assiel.

"Give me your name, woman."

Assiel didn't speak, didn't move, didn't indicate that she had even marked the question.

"Give me your name, woman!"

The great dark dragon eyes bored into Assiel's grey ones.

"I see," said the dragon at long last, and turned away. Her eyes lighted on Eloderaẏ. In caressing tones, she ordered, "Come to me, child."

With jerky movements Eloderaẏ obeyed. The dragon's tongue flicked out and touched Eloderaẏ's cheek.

"Kill your companions."

The will of the dragon had so prevailed over Eloderaẏ that she did not even hesitate. Out of the dead jogen's neck she drew the sword Pluriel had given her, and approached Gonor, still robotically. Gonor stared straight ahead at Nevarra.

Eloderaẏ raised the sword.

*"Horlach fi sakal, tanhnel yelh rẃnh!"*

A great weight disappeared abruptly from Eloderaẏ's shoulders. In horror she looked at the sword she held raised.

"Lower that blade."

The musical voice held an impetus that even the dragon's had not. Eloderaý did as she had been told. Then she looked at Nevarra. The dragon's head was flopped on the ground and the great worm lay stunned. The spell broke audibly.

"Rest and eat," was Assiel's only comment, "and then we shall search the Keep for the Sword of the Star."

The food which they ate seemed very sweet that early misty morning, but at last they put it away and rose to begin their search. They dug through the contents of many chambers permeated with dragon-stench. On the uppermost floor they came to the most malodorous chamber of all: Nevarra's own lair. No great pile of gold filled the room, for Nevarra was not a dragon like those of peasants' tales. Only an ornate chest of pure silver stood in the precise centre. Galdore was about to lift the lid when Assiel stayed him with her hand.

"I shall do it."

It never occurred to him to argue the matter with her. He simply rose from his knees and stood aside. The woman knelt before the chest and effortlessly raised the heavy lid.

Inside lay the Sword of the Star.

It was clear that the blade had originally been pure white, but now it was streaked with bright red veins. From the gold guard the blade tapered to a perfect pinpoint. The two-handed hilt was white too, banded with gold. The very simplicity of its make was what made it the most beautiful sword any of the men present had ever imagined.

"Omnipotent ruler of all the lands of Militer, of the depths of the Great Sea, and of the furthest reaches of the heavens, I have come in answer to your summons. What does my lord command?"

"Nevarra answers not when I call. Ready fifty Flokav to accompany you. When you have them, call me. I will transport you directly to the Keep."

The day passed slowly. Most of the company went to rest at midday, and Pluriel alone stayed with Assiel guarding the Sword, which none of them had touched. Assiel remained in the shadows near the back of the room, and Pluriel sat leaning against the chest, nodding off.

He was nearly asleep when he heard a heavy tread outside the room, and he jerked fully awake. It was probably just one of the others returning, but somehow he felt jumpy. He dropped his eyelids till they were nearly shut and watched the door through the slits.

The door eased open and a figure slipped in – a familiar figure, with whom Pluriel had drunk wine, broken bread, many times.

Eparne saw Pluriel lounging against the chest, apparently asleep, and an evil smirk grew on his face. He crept towards the centre of the room, silently drawing his sword as he went.

Then Pluriel leapt up, whipping out his sword. He thrust at the startled Eparne, who, however, with a deftness born of many years of swordfighting, parried the blow and speedily returned with a crafty attack. They duelled for some time, but Eparne eventually found himself on the losing side. Pluriel, after all, was the most expert swordsman ever to serve under Fortaer's king. Filled with a coward's fear for his life, Eparne whistled shrilly. At once the fifty Flokav streamed into the chamber.

Faced with odds of fifty-one to one, Pluriel spared one instant to see what Assiel was doing.

She had not left her shadowy nook.

"Why aren't you helping me?" he yelled at her, countering attacks from every side. He backed up against a wall to prevent sneak attacks from behind and glanced over the heads of the Flokav. Assiel simply shook her head, wearing one of her inexplicable expressions. Pluriel started, comprehending something.

"Don't you dare kill any of them!"

He had lowered the odds to only twenty-seven to one when Eparne, who'd been standing on the edge of the skirmish, seemed to regain some of his courage. He held up his hand, and the Flokav fell back.

"Let me at him."

The Flokav scattered, and Eparne advanced on Pluriel.

"Now you will die, King's puppet."

"Or perhaps *you* will die, Dark Lord's pawn."

"Oh, I think not."

Their swords clashed together once more. Eparne seemed possessed of an evil spirit, so fiercely did he wield his blade and so contorted was his face. But Pluriel too received strength from some invisible power, and his face was not contorted but brightened and glowing. The fight seemed evenly matched.

Then both men thrust at the same time, each forgetting to guard himself in a desperate attempt to kill his enemy. Pluriel's blade cut through to Eparne's heart; Eparne's lunge drove true to Pluriel's.

The two men fell dead, each with the other's sword buried in him. They had been at one time as brothers; they died the other's mortal foe.

# 14

THE SURVIVING FLOKAV, SEEING THEIR LEADER'S FALL, fled shrieking.

Assiel moved from her corner and bent over Pluriel's body. His face had not lost the radiant shine it had borne; rather, in death it had grown even brighter. His eyes were open and held an expression of deep and perfect peace. Joy seemed to speak from every feature and shadow of that face. Two tears, not salt but fresh, fell from Assiel's grey eyes onto the body.

A voice came up the stairs, accompanied by hastening footsteps. "What on earth is going on?"

Ringard burst into the room. He took in the

corpses of the Flokav lying scattered about the room, then his eyes fixed upon Assiel kneeling on the floor. Ringard had loved his brother better than any other human being. Instinctively now he knew that it was his brother over whom Assiel wept. With a cry of anguish his heart seemed to rip into a thousand tiny pieces. He fell on his knees beside his brother's body, crying aloud to Elamm' in despairing supplication.

When all his grief was drained he raised his head and saw his friends standing silently beside him.

"He always said he would defeat the Dark Lord or die in the attempt," he said numbly. "He is at peace."

He tried to get up then, but stumbled. Galdore took his hands and helped to him his feet. Then he embraced him. No one spoke: speech was unnecessary, and impossible.

At last Ringard looked down at Pluriel's body. "How shall we bury him? I will not leave him in the Swamp."

"We can carry him back to dry land and dig a grave there," said Galdore. "But we must leave soon. How much longer will Nevarra be stunned?"

"It will not be long now," answered Assiel.

"Then I shall carry Pluriel," said Ringard. "Who will take Eparne's body?"

"Do we not leave him here with his Flokav friends?" asked Tristal, shocked at Ringard's words.

"He was almost a brother once," Ringard said softly.

"He *killed* your brother!"

"Would you have me forever carry hate for one who is dead? He also was a creature of Elamm'." Ringard's voice stumbled. "I for one... forgive him."

"I will carry Eparne," said Assiel unexpectedly.

"What about the Sword?" asked Eloderaý. "We're not leaving that."

"No." Assiel walked towards the chest. When she reached it, she turned to face them all. "Not one of you has yet touched this sword, for you have doubted your right to do so. I now claim the right. For the Sword of the Star is mine, and I am Royaleisia the Strong."

Dumbfounded, not one of the company moved as Royaleisia bent to raise the Sword from its place. And then there was a brilliant flash of light, and when they could see again she was clad no longer in the long white gown but in a tunic of white trimmed with gold, and the Sword was buckled about her waist.

"Now come at once," she commanded. "We have little time left." She raised Eparne's body and led the mournful procession down the winding steps of the Keep.

They buried the bodies of Pluriel and Eparne side by side a mile from the Swamp, and Ringard, Pluriel's nearest living relative, spoke the words of farewell.

"Life is but one part of a greater journey, a journey which all must take, to come to know and love Elamm', and serve him with all their being. Death is the latter part of the journey, and perhaps the better, for after death men come face to face with Elamm'. Therefore let the tears of those who remain be brief, and keep ever green and joyful the memories of Pluriel and Eparne."

Then they turned their backs on the Swamp and the graves, and started for Drista, Royaleisia carrying Gonor on her back. They felt they had little time, and Ringard, unanimously elected their new leader, set a speedy pace. He insisted that they must attempt to cover thirty miles a day – the best a trained messenger could do – or they would be too late. And although Tristal and Galdore were inclined to think it too great an expectation, they found that Royaleisia agreed that all haste was imperative, and this stilled all complaints before they were voiced.

They were running hard most of the time, but still in their momentary pauses for a brief morsel of food, they could see that the land was not as a land in spring should be, but rather as a land in autumn. The verdure that they had noticed coming down from the Mountains had been replaced by dying grass and trees which had prematurely lost their plumage. The few flowers they glimpsed were drooping, fading into the wilting grass.

"Jalavak's reach grows longer," Royaleisia said when the company stopped for the first night, having covered twenty miles from the Swamp already. "He is killing the spring of Staran with his touch of death. Ringard was right. Haste is crucial now."

For some time everyone was too weary to speak. Eloderaý went to sleep without even waiting for supper. One by one the rest fell asleep as well, until only Ringard sat awake, guarding the camp, and Royaleisia stood a yard or two from him.

"Things are moving," she said quietly, and Ringard jumped, for he had thought she was asleep, and was nodding off himself."

"What do you mean?" he asked her.

"Leftar of Fortaer is about to attack the Three Towers."

Ringard leapt up, now fully alert. "Is he mad?"

"No," she replied. "He has been told to do this."

"By what mad fool?"

She turned to look at him. "By Elamm'."

Horrified by his own words, Ringard sat down and buried his face in his hands. He quelled a desire to rage about in despair. His world was falling apart around him: his brother was dead; King Leftar, like a second father, was surely going to die. And Jalavak was already veiling his beloved Staran in death. What use was it to go on?

He sat staring into the dark. Finally he spoke without looking at Royaleisia.

"What happens to those who die?"

"I have never died," she replied softly, a smile in her voice.

"But you must know, at the least, what

happens after death. You are a Valintara."

Royaleisia's smile died, then recovered, and she spoke quietly but with a certain joy. "After a man's death, he knows the most perfect joy. He meets Elamm' and is reunited with dead family members, and is given perfect knowledge. For the just, death is nothing to fear. But..." Her tone darkened ominously. "But those with evil thoughts in their hearts are cast into an endless Void of darkness, more terrible than any tongue can describe."

She fell silent. Ringard shuddered. Then, hesitantly, almost unwillingly, he asked a question.

"And what of those who have repented of their evil?"

The question hung quivering in the air, asking and re-asking itself, until Royaleisia replied.

"They go through a period of restitution for the damage they have done. Then they, too, enter into the perfect and everlasting joy."

# 15

Lalethiel entered her husband's tent. King Leftar sat at a low table, studying a battle plan and occasionally taking an absent-minded bite of the slice of bread which lay on a plate beside him. The Queen joined him at the table and began to rub his shoulders.

"Kanethon should be here!" he fretted. "We've been waiting three days! Surely he should be here by now."

"Calm yourself," she said. "It takes time for a messenger to reach Drista, and then Kanethon has still to muster his army and get them all to Drista in readiness to march. Staran is a large country, my love. And after that, they still have nearly forty leagues to cross to Evilka."

"I know, I know," he muttered, returning his attention to the plan before him. Lalethiel began to wander around the tent, restlessly flipping through a book that lay on the cot.

The flap of the tent opened and Celodhel, Leftar's second-in-command since Eparne's disappearance some time ago, came in. He took in the King's engrossed attitude and the Queen's fidgety one, and instead of interrupting either stood restively in the background.

"Well, what is it, Celodhel?" asked Leftar irritably, gaze still focussed on the parchment.

Celodhel strode forward and knelt before the King. "My lord King, we either attack now, or be attacked. It may be as little as a few hours, or as much as a few days, but for a half hour a steady stream of Flokav has been pouring into Tolemka."

"You *fool!*" cried the King, overturning the table and leaping up. "You *fool!* Why didn't you come to me at once?"

Celodhel flushed and fiddled with the end of his belt, but King Leftar ignored him except insofar as to push past him out of the tent.

"Where is my standard-bearer?" he

demanded of one of the guards.

"Here, my lord King," and a man came out from behind the tent.

"Blow the muster at once, Amarl," Leftar ordered him. "I want every single man ready to start the attack in two hours at most."

"But my lord King, sixteen thousand men cannot prepare so quickly!"

"They must!"

"I... can't... keep going," Elodera rasped, trying to catch a full breath. "It feels... as though... my throat is ripping... apart."

Ringard slowed. "We'll stop for dinner, then – but we won't stop long."

In relief, Elodera dropped to the ground and lay still. The others dug into their packs for food.

"My supply is getting pretty low," said Tristal as he removed his bundle of *marcin*. He counted the cakes. "I've got enough for maybe four or five days."

"I still have plenty," said Galdore, "so I can share if you need it." His eyes twinkled. "You really shouldn't eat so much."

Tristal smirked. "Considering we've been

running from sun-up to sundown for three days, I'd think I had a right to eat like a giant!"

"We've only got about five days left if we keep this pace," stated Ringard flatly, effectively squashing the banter. "Eat as much as you need to, Tristal; you can't hold us up. Eloderaý!"

"Mm," she replied, her face in the grass.

"What I just said goes for you too. If you or Tristal holds us up, we leave you behind. Now get up. Haven't you even eaten yet?"

She flushed but held her tongue, unwilling to fray his taut emotions any further. Easing into a sitting position, she crammed a cake of *marcin* into her mouth. "Now I have."

Jalavak's army was at least ten times the size of Leftar's, yet the King of Fortaer held his own. His losses were not light; in five days he had lost as many thousand men, yet the enemy's forces had somehow been ravaged even more devastatingly.

The Queen still fought at her husband's side – she had not left him once. As a jogen charged at the pair, wildly brandishing a dirk, they fought it together and brought it down swiftly. It fell, legs rather than sword flailing this time. As it dropped to the ground, its dirk went flying and lodged itself in the back of a Floka. Then the couple was separated as several Flokav rushed them at once. Lalethiel was as adept in swordplay as her husband, perhaps more so, for the innate grace in her movements turned the fight into a dance.

All at once there came a cry from behind Queen Lalethiel. Instinctively she whirled, unintentionally beheading a Floka with her outstretched blade. Leftar was down on his back, kicking at a beast which was leaning over him, its drooling jaws gaping wide. Never before had Lalethiel seen such a creature. Grey it was, with a wolf's snout, but black stripes streaked across its back, like a halfbreed wolf-tiger. And it was as large as a draft horse.

The beast gave a long drawn-out howl like a wolf's, and it snapped at the King's face.

Lalethiel shrieked. "Look here, you brute! Look at me! Come and kill me!"

"Lalethiel, no!" shouted Leftar.

The animal took a second to look round at her with interest.

"Yes, me! Not him, me!"

It turned back to Leftar, but Lalethiel

screamed again.

"Over here, you stupid brute!"

First it killed the King. Then it obeyed the Queen.

It bowled her over, but she managed to keep a grip on her sword. As the beast lunged towards her face, she brought up the sword and the creature impaled itself. It gave a horrible wail and flopped backward.

The Queen struggled up, but her husband was dead. She collapsed on his chest and closed her eyes against a pain she noticed only now. The thing had clawed her.

It was twenty minutes later when Prince Kedýran by chance fought through to the place where his parents lay. With a terrible drop of his heart he saw them. His father was gone, but the Queen was alive.

Barely alive.

"*Alahs!*" he whispered.

She opened her eyes and recognised her son. "Kedýran," she murmured, "*dẃnhl nelach....*"

"Have no worries for my father," he told her, tears in his eyes.

"No, I know he is dead, *sularh amh*. What I wish to say – " She heaved a gasp. "He acted... under Elamm's... guidance. You... are King now.

Regroup your army. Perhaps Kanethon..." Her voice faded. "...will come. Jalavak... will."

He remained on his knees at her side, weeping aloud, cradling her head in his arms.

"*Sariënh, rohelin sularh amh,*" she whispered, and her head fell back.

*Farewell, my beloved son.*

# 16

ON THE SEVENTH DAY OF THEIR JOURNEY SOUTH, Eloderaÿ's sharp eyes caught sight of a golden haze somewhere ahead of them. She pointed, and Ringard nodded.

"Only a league left," he commented.

Eloderaÿ looked at him again and frowned. His conversation had become uncharacteristically terse. And he never smiled. Assiel's eyes followed him often, her feelings indecipherable, but he didn't speak to her – he rarely spoke to anyone lately. But Assiel had voiced no comment, and it was hardly Eloderaÿ's place to say anything herself.

"The Golden Castle of Staran!" breathed Galdore in awe as they reached the gates just over an hour later. "It is rightly named in the old tales!"

"I've heard it's made entirely of gold," said Tristal, "and gems are lavishly embedded in the walls."

"That would be an exaggeration," muttered Ringard. "Although it is the most beautiful thing in all Militer. I grew up here after my parents' deaths." He cleared his throat and turned to the sentry who stepped up to them.

"What want you here?" His words were rough, and his countenance the same – clearly a common soldier elevated in time of need to the position of watchman. "Answer me, strangers!"

"I am no stranger here," replied Ringard curtly. "I am Ringard son of Frosindal, cousin of Lord Elwyn and friend to the King. I bring him urgent tidings."

The man's face cleared. "I have heard of you," he said, bowing shallowly, "and your brother Pluriel." Seeing a shadow of pain cross Ringard's face, he cut himself short. "But the King is not here. Not three hours ago he rode out with the army to Fortaer."

Ringard's eyes filled with thunder, but he spoke in a carefully guarded tone. "It is critical that I see him. Do you have horses for us?"

The guard shifted his weight onto his left leg. "I don't have the authority, but based on your name I will risk lending you the swiftest horses left in the stables." His eyes narrowed. "If it turns out you're lying about your name, I will hunt you down and you will pay."

Ringard gave a nod. "Thank you."

Most of the horses left behind were sickly or old, but there were some that were well enough to be ridden, and four were all Ringard asked for. Eloderaý was furious.

"I can ride behind one of you!" she protested. "I don't *want* to be left behind! I have just as much right to fight as any man, and if I die no one will care!"

Ringard held up a hand to stop her flow of words. "I am responsible for you, Eloderaý, and you will do as I say." He turned his back on her and strode towards the courtyard where the stableboys were saddling the horses.

She followed. "I don't want to be left here like an annoying piece of extra baggage that has to wait till everyone important is finished doing everything exciting. I'm old enough to make my own decisions! And Pluriel was my friend too. Can't I do something for his memory too?"

A flash of pain lit Ringard's face, and she knew she had gone too far, but he only said, "You will stay here," before turning away. "How fast are they going?" he asked the guard as they mounted the horses.

"I heard they were making as much speed as they can."

Galdore calculated swiftly. "They could be three leagues gone by now."

"Ride hard!" ordered Ringard.

The unlucky horses were pushed to their outer extreme, yet it took over four hours to draw near the tail end of the column. It was another quarter hour before they drew level with the King's guard at the head of the line.

"My lord!" shouted Ringard as he glimpsed Kanethon in the midst of his guard. Kanethon turned round but, not seeing Ringard, did not stop. Ringard shouted again. Then one of the royal guard recognised him and called out to the King. Kanethon reined in his horse and gradually the entire army came to a halt.

"Ringard!" cried the King, riding through the

men clustered around him.

Ringard jerked his head toward the soldiers, who were clearly interested in what was going on. "Can we speak privately?"

Kanethon nodded. "Although you will have to be brief. I fear we are already too late." He rode toward a copse of trees and Ringard rode after him, motioning for his friends to follow.

"Where's your brother?" asked Kanethon as soon as they were alone.

"Dead," Ringard said bluntly – and bitterly. "But that is another tale." He briefly told the gist of the quest. "We have the Sword – Assiel has it." He turned round to introduce Royaleisia, but she was nowhere in sight.

"Assiel?" The King stared at Ringard.

A tic animated Ringard's brow. "My lord, there is no time to explain. She will return when she needs to."

"I will trust your judgement," Kanethon replied. "Hopeless or not, we will come to the aid of Leftar."

"Our mounts are weary, my lord," put in Tristal. "I am not sure that they can carry us much longer."

"We must push them on till they drop dead of

weariness, son!" The King wheeled his horse about, and with one signal from his hand the army moved once more.

Eloderaý was left to her own devices after a few old matrons had their fill of fussing over her. This particular afternoon, her idea of a few well-spent hours was snooping around, for she had come up with an idea which she thought ingenious. Bare feet flapping on the cold flagstones, she padded down dark deserted hallways. At the meeting of two corridors she met a dead end, a heavy oaken door. She gave it a half-hearted shove and a kick, then leaned against it trying to get her bearings.

An old maid hurried past, and Eloderaý called out before she disappeared.

She halted. "Yes, child?"

"What's past this door?"

"That's the armoury, dear."

*Perfect.* The maid went on, and Eloderaý smirked. She listened carefully for a moment, then placed her hands on the door and pushed with all her strength. The door, however, yielded not an inch. She squeezed her eyes shut and strained, and it gave a horrible squealing creak as it opened a tiny crack. Eloderaý stood back, panting. Then she set her shoulder against the door and eased the door open just far enough to slip through.

Her footsteps echoed against the walls and across the high vaulted ceiling. Light fell from two windows on the far side of the room, disclosing a nearly empty armoury. She rooted through what the army had left and finally found a small-sized mail hauberk and leather breastplate, perhaps a boy's toy armour. Near the hauberk and breastplate she discovered one pair of boots that were not far too large – stout leather boots plated with metal, just lower than her knees.

It was sheer luck that she didn't meet anyone on her way back to her room, since there was no conceivable way of hiding her loot. She stashed it under her bed, then descended to the kitchen in hopes of supper. Her tray was liberally filled, and what she didn't eat immediately she stored for her journey.

Under cover of dark she crept to the stables, where she donned the hauberk and boots. The breastplate she found was impossible to manage on her own, but she strapped it to the saddle of her horse and hoped she would find a way of putting it on when she needed it. She swathed the horse's hooves in cloth and led it quietly across the courtyard. Once through the gate, she unwrapped its hooves, swung up onto the horse's back, and cantered away.

She was nearly a league from Drista when a disembodied voice came out of the night.

"Stop!"

Eloderaý gave a terrified scream. Spooked, her horse reared up, and she flailed and lost her seat. A hand reached out and picked her up.

"Who are you?" she whispered, still frightened out of her wits.

A torch flared. Eloderaý almost sobbed in relief as she recognised Royaleisia.

"If we are not quick we will be too late."

"You sound as though you expected me!" exclaimed Eloderaý.

"I returned for you," Royaleisia replied. "You are needed in Fortaer."

"*I* am needed? Where are the others?"

"Suffice to say that they are not here. There is no time now to explain – you must trust me."

She gave Eloderaý a hand remounting her horse, and together they rode south-westwards across the withering meadows of Staran.

# 17

INTO MALARN STREAMED THE FORTAEREN ARMY, A long string of filthy and exhausted soldiers. Nearly the entire city had turned out to witness their return, but none cheered. With solemn faces they surveyed the tattered remnants of the army that had so proudly left Malarn only a fortnight before. They watched miserably as the prince separated from the rest and mounted a dais to speak. He had no glad words for them despite their victory. He told of the deaths of the King and Queen; he told of the thousands of men who had fallen. He admonished them to refresh themselves quickly before strengthening their fortifications, for Jalavak's retaliation could not be long in coming.

Had any then been close enough to look into the prince's face, he would have seen only hopelessness.

As Kedýran stepped down from the platform someone cried out, "All hail our King!" A few voices weakly took up the shout, but few had enough enthusiasm to join in, and al cheers died into nothingness.

The prince stumbled as he began to climb the steps, and a guard leaped forward to support him. Had Kedýran eighteen years? His stature suggested seventy as he crept into the palace, leaning on the guard's arm.

"Where is my cousin?" he murmured as they seated him on a soft couch.

"He has been away for days, my lord," replied the guard. "He went east, but beyond that no one knows where."

"Find him for me," whispered Kedýran, lying back and closing his eyes. Softly everyone left the room.

Hours later a maid came in to clean and found him fast asleep, his eyes buttoned tightly shut – the way they'd always done since he was a baby.

He was lying on his side and his cheek was cupped in the palm of his hand. Contrasted against a dark pillow, his white face looked so terribly young. She stole back out, careful not to wake him.

Dawn was nigh when Kedýran started awake, both his mind and his body refreshed by the dreamless sleep. Neither grief nor anger possessed him now: only a grim and determined purpose. Never would he yield his people to the Dark Lord, not through a whining surrender, not through a lost battle! He was King of Fortaer; he would be crowned that day; he would lead his people to victory, or they would all fall in a defeat of which songs might be made.

The mood of the city had improved with a night's sleep, and not only the whole of Malarn but also peasants from the outlying farms came to see Kedýran crowned that afternoon. Having a crowned ruler again put brief hope in their hearts, and they hailed their new King lustily. But by nightfall a pall had settled once more on the city, and the streets were silent.

The next day began early as the children and most of the women were sent into the country-side and hidden in the caves behind the Falls of the Great River. All day long the air was filled with the sounds of the construction of a wall around the front of the city. Kedýran himself worked alongside the men, and it was late ere he fell wearily into his bed.

But he was woken soon after by an abrupt knock on the door of his bedchamber and an urgent call of "My lord!"

He sat, rubbing sleep out of his eyes, and invited the knocker in. His voice did not carry its most inviting tone but the door opened and two figures entered.

"My lord, you asked for your cousin, Lord Eparne. He is here."

Kedýran jumped up eagerly, all fatigue gone, and was about to embrace his cousin, but Eparne rebuffed him with a brief "No time for greetings." He looked to the servant. "Leave us."

With a bow he was obeyed. Eparne took a seat on Kedýran's desk, his demeanour ruffled.

"Now listen carefully to me, cousin. I've come with an important message for you. When Lord Jalavak comes to Malarn, you are not to antagonise him. Keep your men within the walls of the city. You yourself must go out and speak with him. We must come to a peaceful conclusion, without more bloodshed."

"You think Jalavak would make an agreement with me?" said Kedýran, shocked. "You think the Dark Lord will be reasonable?"

"No, no, Kedýran! Lord Jalavak is not a Dark Lord, but a king like yourself, only more powerful than you will ever be. May not two kings come to an agreement? Fortaer must submit to Lord Jalavak, and hope for clemency despite your father's ill-advised and unprovoked assault."

"Ill-advised?" Kedýran grew hot with anger. "Ill-advised, when it was commanded by Elamm' himself?"

Eparne scowled. "Where do you get that idea, Kedýran?"

"At one time, I might have told you, cousin. But you are not yourself tonight. Take rest now, and we will speak more in the morning."

Eparne rose from his seat on the desk.

"You are a fool, King of Fortaer, and a pompous fool. We will not speak in the morning, nor ever again, unless perchance we meet in the afterlife."

Outraged, Kedýran started up, but Eparne's form wavered, then disintegrated into nothing. A hateful hiss came from behind Kedýran, and he spun around as the sound echoed through the chamber. All at once filled with terror, Kedýran stumbled backwards and fell onto his bed, gasping. The hiss grew to a shriek and he covered his ears.

The door burst open and three guards burst in.

"My lord!" two of them cried simultaneously.

"A wraith!" the King shouted, "an evil wraith it was! My cousin is dead and Jalavak has conjured up his wraith to tempt me!"

Uncomprehending, none of the men moved, but stood stock still, staring at their King.

When Kedýran woke in the early morning after a few hours' troubled sleep, he thought at first that it was still night, for no light came through the windows. He slid off his bed, made his way across the room to look out, stretching his aching arms. A fleecy blanket of thick storm clouds swathed the sky and little sunlight was able to filter through. Feeling something ominous in the quiet air, he dressed swiftly and left his chamber.

The palace corridors were alive with frenzied haste; men ran back and forth, some clanking in full mail, some clinking in half a suit of armour, and some in ordinary apparel. No one seemed to notice the King as he pushed his way through the masses.

Finally Kedýran saw a face he knew – the captain of the King's Guard. "Ealcar!" he shouted.

The captain turned and, recognizing Kedýran, approached him at once.

"Ealcar, what is the meaning of all this?"

"My lord, you must come at once to see!" Ealcar's expression was a mixture of fear, anger, and a kind of excitement as he led Kedýran out of the palace. The two men ran down the street, which was absolutely empty and still; through the square, and up onto the gate of the city. Kedýran was shocked to see that only overnight, an army had appeared on the plain before the city; the field was swarming with Flokav and jogens and wolgers – the name the Fortaerim had given to the crossbreed beast of the Battle of Tolemka.

He turned around and stood with a dazed appearance staring out into the square.

"Get down, m'lord!" one of the gatekeepers

shouted of a sudden, and Ealcar shoved him to the ground, then fell beside him with a thud.

Kedýran rolled over onto his back and stared up at the sky.

"Don't get up," ordered the gatekeeper, now down on his front himself. "Slide over to the steps and get off this gate, but whatever ya do, don't put your head up over the wall!"

Kedýran obeyed without questioning, standing up when he reached the cobblestones again. "What happened?"

The gatekeeper did not reply till he was standing beside Kedýran on the ground. "A Floka shot at ya, musta known somehow you were the King."

Kedýran looked back up at the gate. "And Ealcar took the arrow for me." Looking up at the gate, he could see the red fletching on the arrow. His brow contracted. "Prepare for battle," he ordered those nearby. He strode back up to the palace. The captain of the Palace Division met him as he was going into the palace.

"Your orders, my lord?"

"All men must arm themselves at once!"

Close on five hundred archers covered every foot of the front battlement of the city; below them in the square were row upon row of foot soldiers. They could not see what was happening outside, but they could hear brute shouts as the Flokav prepared their devilry. Some fretted with the delay; others felt fear overtaking them and wished that they were at home. All nature was perfectly subdued, as though it sensed an imminent and inevitable end.

At length there came cheers from the Flokav. Then the battering ram smashed into the gate. The wood splintered, throwing slivers all over the men, and the nose of the ram peeped through before retreating. Some of the archers stumbled, regained their balance, and shot downwards. Several screams drifted up, but twice more the gate was hit. Then the hideous front of the black thing, shaped in a likeness of Jalavak's head, crashed through a yawning aperture. The soldiers shuddered and fell back with terror in their eyes.

"Hold your ground!" cried Kedýran. "Fear no evil! Hold your ground!"

One more time the battering ram struck, and the gate yielded completely. Flokav poured through and met the Fortaerim with a clash. It was impossible to hold for long; Jalavak's horde outnumbered the other by far.

Many men had fallen before, above the shrieks of battle and death, the sweet notes of a horn floated through the air, and its fresh resonance seemed to brighten the earth despite the oppressive storm clouds. Hope returned to the hearts of the Fortaerim as they realized that at last the Startern had come, for no enemy horn could make so pure a music.

"Like Fianë of old, Kanethon comes to turn the tide!" someone cried, and his words were taken up by a great part of the soldiers.

The Flokav on the other hand quailed at the sound of the horn and were soon driven from the city. At the head of the army rode King Kedýran, and he slew all that hindered his course.

At last the fortune of the battle seemed turned from Jalavak. Thousands of Flokav were slain and even jogens and wolgers could not impede the Fortaerim as they swept over the field. But Jalavak could not suffer such a defeat, and he had one other means if all else failed him.

As Kedýran and Kanethon met and greeted one other, a silence of horror fell over all present, friend and enemy alike. Marvelling at this sudden calm, the two kings turned as one. Facing them was one like to a man, but greater in size, swathed entirely in a cloak of startling red, his face hidden. Kanethon's horse reared in terror and took off. His wrist still in Kanethon's grasp, Kedýran was jerked from his own mount, which fled at once.

For a moment he lay motionless in the dust, the breath knocked totally from him. He gasped a couple times, recovering himself, then slowly rose, retrieving his sword from where it had fallen. Hate filled his eyes as he stood before the apparition.

"Now, you die."

Jalavak's voice was not so unlike to Royaleisia's own. But no song was this to give pleasure, though it was smooth and syrupy; this was a song of menace and hate and subjugating fury, a song of beauty and love gone awry.

No shudder, however, did the King give, nor did he cower away. With the all-encompassing hate staring out of his pale blue eyes he faced the Dark Lord without flinching.

With an invisible movement Jalavak rid himself of his cloak. Unable to look into that awful face, against his will Kedýran moved his arm to block the sight of him. Jalavak stretched out one arm towards Kedýran, and he dropped to the ground, instantly killed.

Ignoring the petrified Fortaeren soldiers nearby, Jalavak turned to the city and surveyed it with expressionless, colourless eyes. Smoke rose from the eastern quarter just behind the gate, and it was spreading.

# 18

THE SUN DAWNED OVER ROYALEISIA AND ELODERAÝ, and the latter gasped as she saw for the first time the Mountains of Fortaer, crowned with the pink sunrise. The two women were riding alongside the outermost bases of the mountains, and Eloderaý had to tip her head so far back to see the peaks that it made her dizzy and nauseous, causing her to look back down again swiftly.

"It is beautiful, is it not?" Royaleisia called back. "But soon we must delve down beneath their roots."

Excitement stabbed through Eloderaý.

"We're going in a cave?"

Royaleisia reined in her horse, quickly dismounted, and helped Elorderaý slide off her seat. She spoke in a whisper to both of the horses, and at once they took off, galloping towards the south. Then Elorderaý followed Royaleisia to a massive boulder, one smooth, flat side of which rose eight feet into the air.

Royaleisia set her palms against the rockface and began to murmur words which Elorderaý could not catch. Slowly a crack appeared in the rock, running across and downwards to form a rectangular shape, seven feet tall and four wide. A tremor seemed to pass from Royaleisia's hands into the rock, and it slowly revolved on an unseen hinge to reveal an aperture through which a man both tall and broad might pass.

"Come," said Royaleisia, and Elorderaý tiptoed after her through the doorway.

About five steps from the door, a flight of stone stairs led down into the earth. As Royaleisia set her foot on the first of these, the door behind them silently revolved again, shutting out the daylight. Elorderaý expected Royaleisia to light a torch, but she did not; rather, at frequent intervals along the roof of stone, a rock glowed, giving off a soft dim light that was enough to see by.

The steps seemed endless, but as Eloderaý was beginning to feel she could not survive another three stairs at most, Royaleisia came to a halt at the bottom of the steps. As Royaleisia closed her eyes and appeared to be thinking about something, Eloderaý looked around. To her left, there was only a stone wall, but in front of her and to her right there was a colossal open cave, roofed by a stone dome. All the cave was bathed with light of a colour which Eloderaý had never before experienced, and she could never say afterwards to which known colour it had seemed most similar – she thought it was completely unfamiliar and did not resemble any earthly hue.

To Eloderaý's right, one flight of steps led to a lower level where she could see gems studding the stone of the walls and floor; beside the wall of the cave more stairs led yet further down into the earth. Before her, an arched bridge spanned an abyss in the depths of which more gems twinkled up. The bridge was four, perhaps five, feet wide, and without a railing or handhold; and it was here that Royaleisia led Eloderaý. As the

Valintara stepped onto the bridge, however, she paused.

"I sense an evil that ought not to penetrate to this place," she said quietly.

"What *is* this place?" asked Eloderaý.

"This is an ancient earthly stronghold of the Valintari," Royaleisia explained, continuing onto the bridge. "Here the only power present should be that of Elamm', yet I feel a different power also." Now she seemed to be talking to herself and not to Eloderaý, but she made no attempt to prevent the girl from hearing her words. "Yes, it seems weak enough, but it ought not to be present at all!" She turned back to her companion. "Keep your voice low and use caution in all that you do here."

Eloderaý nodded, and they moved on.

The opposite side of the bridge widened out into a narrow ledge beyond which was a tunnel, narrow and tall. As the two entered the passageway, the light dimmed considerably; the glowing stones in the roof were no longer regularly placed. Now there was only just enough light to see a couple feet ahead. Nervously Eloderaý placed a hand on the wall and kept it there.

They travelled down the tunnel for a time, then Royaleisia turned left, then right, then quickly another left. Eloderaý trotted after her, trying to keep up with her brisk pace. At length they turned into a small hollowed-out cave, affording room for only three people or so.

"Here we can take a few hours' rest," Royaleisia told Eloderaý, and with relief the latter lowered her weary body to the cave floor. She soon fell into a deep sleep of utter exhaustion, but Royaleisia remained sitting alertly near the entrance to the cave, her eyes wide open and staring straight ahead.

Three hours later, Eloderaý started awake and sat up. Her back ached from her hard bed and there was a crick in her neck. She shook her head a little, clearing the dizziness from her eyes, and tried to accustom her vision to the darkness. She could see barely anything.

"Royaleisia?" she said quietly.

There was no answer, and Eloderaý repeated herself. Still nothing. A nervous fear travelled from her stomach to her throat and tried to choke her, but she swallowed it and rose to her feet. It was so dark that standing made her feel giddy again, and as she could see nothing it felt as though the small cave in which she stood felt huge. That nervousness that one feels when one is alone in a pitch-black expanse of who knows what size, swelled up and tried to overcome her.

"Royaleisia?" she said a third time.

"Out here," replied a voice, and Eloderaý could have cried in relief to find that she was not alone in the darkness. With one hand touching the wall to guide herself, she crept fumblingly around the cave until she found the opening into the tunnel.

"Come," said the voice again. "Follow my voice."

She obeyed, following the sound of the words. After some time she glimpsed a soft light in the distance, and it grew as they came closer. Finally Eloderaý found herself in another cave, perhaps thirty feet square – but apparently alone.

"Where are you?" she asked.

"Here," said the voice, and Eloderaý turned to her left. But it was not Royaleisia who stood there.

"Where is Royaleisia?" she cried.

The piercing eyes of the man drilled into her own, and she fell back shuddering. Then she realized something. "You are the man who captured Tristal in Tarcap!" After a moment she recognized him a second time. "And you killed Pluriel in Duskmoor Keep," she added in a low tone.

And then she remembered a third thing which she knew about this man. And she screamed. The sound reverberated back and forth, echoing off the walls, and travelling up and down the passageways that led away from the cave.

"And Pluriel killed me in Duskmoor Keep," the man said cheerfully.

"You... are a... wraith." She had to force the words out, so great was her dread.

"So shall you be, my sweet," he said, and stepped toward her.

She screamed again and turned, fumbling around in a futile attempt to escape. The soft light went out, and all that enabled her to see Eparne's continued approach was an eerie greenish light that surrounded him entirely. Her eyes were fixed on his face, but she heard him draw a dagger from a sheath at his waist.

"Do you know what this knife can do?" he asked her, not pausing his steps. When she did not reply, he smiled mockingly. "This blade is from the land of the condemned dead. A Void-blade it is, and when I drive it into your heart you shall die. But you shall not rest; no, for all eternity you shall not rest but shall be driven unceasingly to the four corners of the earth and back."

He held the dagger up and ran his finger along the edge of the blade, his eyes ever-fixed upon her face.

"Shall you like to join me, my sweet?"

His gaze, however, had not quite the same hypnotizing power as Nevarra's, and Eloderaý retained her will and the ability to think, though in stunted form. She knew there was something she ought to be remembering, but the spell upon her was strong enough to enchain that of her knowledge which might enable her to break the spell or to save herself, unless she had the strength to wrestle it to the forefront of her mind.

She closed her eyes, swaying a little, and exerted all her strength towards recalling this memory. And here was the undoing of the hypnotism, for she knew that she had before experienced something of its sort, and her mind irresistibly went back to Duskmoor Keep and the dragon-spell. And then she thought of the jogens, and her fight with one of them. And... and... what was that elusive detail?

Her eyes flew open and she whipped out the sword Pluriel had given her. The momentum drove the sword upward and through Eparne's wrist. But there was only a brief sizzling, and Eparne did not stop. Despairing, Eloderaý realized that she could do nothing against the wraith. Her mind shrieked at her as terrified despair swept through her entire person.

*You're going to die! Become a wraith! Unliving and undead! The dagger...*

The dagger!

Again she snapped back into herself and drove her despair away from her. At least if this last resort failed she would die – or not die – as befitted a warrior.

Through blinding tears of mingled despair and hope she saw Eparne but a few steps from where she stood. She raised her sword, and he laughed a cruel laugh of delight in her fate. She clenched her teeth and leapt forward. With a ringing clang her blade hit the dagger, and it at least was material, for it flew from Eparne's hand and clattered to the ground several yards away.

As Eparne's wraith stood still, stunned by a development that had never been accounted for,

Eloderaý turned and fled from the cave, down one of the tunnels leading from it. Glancing back once, she saw the wraith gliding after her, still surrounded by that horrible green glow.

*Faster, faster!* her brain screamed at her, and she tried to increase her speed, but *Stop, stop!* another part of her mind contradicted the first impulse. A ripping sensation was torturing her lungs, and her steps became stumbling. Only a couple days ago she had been so proud of her newfound running powers, but now fear and hopelessness and darkness all came together to hold her back.

And then she wasn't running anymore; her feet touched nothing, and she was falling, falling into an inky black, and then she was hitting an invisible lake with a painful impact. And she was falling, still falling, and she couldn't breathe, she couldn't think, she was dying. And then there was something struggling to manifest itself in her thoughts, but she was too dizzy, and it would hurt her to let herself think, and she tried to keep the something out of her thoughts. And then the something won out, and the something spoke in a voice that she knew.

*You can do it, love.*

Then she remembered days long ago when she was a child of eight years, and her father was teaching her to swim in a lake. It was cold, and Eloderaý protested and wanted to get out, but no, she must learn to swim. At last *Dẃnhl* was satisfied with her progress, and Eloderaý climbed out of the water to eat her dinner, but *Dẃnhl* and *Alahs* wanted to swim longer, so she sat watching them splashing and racing each other through the water. And suddenly there was a great heaving in the middle of the lake, and the waves grew enormous, and *Dẃnhl* and *Alahs* stopped laughing and swam for the shore; but something black came up from the depths and fell upon her father and mother, and they disappeared, and Eloderaý was screaming and screaming, and next thing she knew she was waking up in a hard cot at Mistress Stellatin's.

*You can do it, love.*

And at the sound of her father's voice that she had not heard for seven years, her arms began to work without being told, and all the air in her lungs was gone and she was going to give up, when suddenly her head burst out onto the surface of the underground lake, and she gulped in huge breaths of sweet air.

# 19

Malarn was lost.

Jalavak swept up the road towards the palace, felling all the Fortaerim who stood in his way. He came to the palace and stood gazing at it. Then he climbed the steps and entered.

All that day Flokav swarmed through Malarn and its palace. The Fortaeren symbols and flags were torn from the walls and battlements, and red flags with the sign of the Three Towers were put in their place. More Flokav set fires throughout the city, finishing the task that the siege had begun. By night Malarn was a smouldering city of ruins, excepting only the palace, which yet stood at the west side of the city, washed in the pink light of evening.

In the palace Jalavak feasted upon the King's stores, and the harsh cries and raucous yells of the triumphant Flokav filled every chamber. All that was beautiful was smashed and destroyed and made hideous with symbols of evil. Kedýran's body was taken and set in the great hall, and they mocked it. Throughout the night the horrid celebration carried on, and the revellers defiled the city.

The sun set over Fortaer.

Treading water, Eloderaý searched through the darkness for any sign of light, or of the wraith, but she could see nothing. She hardly dared to hope that Eparne would not return, but maybe she could find a way out of the lake before he found her there.

But how could she get out? This lake could be vast, and she might die of cold or weariness, or hunger or thirst before she found the end. Or the walls around it could be many feet high, all the same height as the one off which she had fallen. But there was nothing for it but to start searching. She began to swim, her limbs slowly remembering the movements they had learned so many years before. She moved cautiously to prevent striking her head if she reached a wall.

Every so often she stopped to rest, treading water or simply hanging in the water. She had done this perhaps five times when she started again and almost immediately her left hand slapped against a surface of stone rather than liquid. On aching arms she pulled herself out and collapsed on the floor of the cave.

Much, much after, she awoke again and felt herself refreshed but very hungry and parched. Her mouth was crying for water, and she had not the willpower to refuse it despite not knowing what might be in the lake. She leaned over the edge and slurped up mouthful after mouthful of water. Then sitting down again, she dug blindly in her pack for food, coming upon a cake of *marcin*. It was damp and soggy, but to Eloderaý it was the most delicious thing she had ever tasted.

As she finished, she was wondering where she might get to from here when she noticed a light shining in the distance. This reassured her that a path led away from where she was, but what might she find when she reached the light? And her sword, her gift from Pluriel, was lost, probably at the bottom of the lake where she would never find it.

But she had only two choices, to leave soon, or to starve where she was or not far away. She chose the former. Hugging the side of the tunnel leading to the light, she edged along till she came near the light. Then she dropped to her stomach and squirmed to a position where she could see what she might find.

The chamber was empty of life... but the light, oh, the light! It was natural light, streaming in through portholes in the ceiling. It flooded the chamber with warmth, and, without meaning to, Eloderaý entered and stood beneath one of the portholes, turning her face upwards; the sun bathed it, and she closed her eyes for the pleasure of it.

When at last she made herself move, for she must somehow find either Royaleisia or the way out, she took in the rest of the chamber's contents. A stone seat stood in each of the eight corners, for the room's shape was octagonal, and in the centre was a stone table, the sides etched with runes which Eloderaý did not recognise. Feeling somehow awed, she stepped up to the table. A sword lay on it, exactly centred, as far as she could tell. She reached out one finger to touch it, and a slight shock ran through her finger, up her arm, and through her chest till it reached the area of her heart. There it stopped and a warm sensation radiated out through her body. Something stirred within her, and she raised the sword and wrapped her fingers around the handgrip, holding the sword firmly. She stared at the weapon. She felt a strange courage filling her heart, and she even thought she might face Jalavak himself and defeat even him.

Suddenly she became nervous, and quickly she set the sword back down as near its original position as she could, and stepped back from the table.

"Does its power frighten you?"

Eloderaý whirled, and saw one who looked like a man, but he was taller than a human, and his face was more fair, and his voice brought to mind Royaleisia's. The voice of this being, however, carried in it a power that even hers did not, a power to command, though not to dominate.

"My lord, it does."

A kind smile broke out on the Valintara's face, a smile with more beauty even than the beauty of the heavens. He approached, passed by her where she stood a step from the table, and picked up the sword himself. His hands, gripping the sword, were large and bronzed, but somehow they seemed delicate at the same time.

He turned back to her as she was pondering this.

"This is the sword of Kanadh."

"The sword of Courage," she murmured in reply, remembering what she had learned of the Valintari. "And you are Kanadh."

He smiled again. Then he bent down to her height and took one of her hands in his, wrapping the fingers around the handgrip. "My child, I give this sword to you."

"To... to *me*?"

"To you," he repeated. "May you bear it faithfully, and may it give you courage in the great tasks which lie ahead."

"My lord," she said, "what great tasks could I perform?"

A third time Kanadh smiled, and in answer he took her face in his hands and kissed her forehead. And when she had recovered from the touch of a Valintara, he was gone and she was alone again, holding the sword of Kanadh.

And then a soft step startled her, and when she turned around, Royaleisia was standing before her, a sad look in her storm-grey eyes.

"It is time for us to leave," was all she said, and Eloderaý followed her from the chamber without a question.

*She had felt herself drawn irresistibly to the Western Gate; she felt Kanadh's presence and sensed his calling to her. She could not complete her task without seeing him one last time. She stood in the sunlight just outside the Gate and waited for him. It was not long before he came, and at once they were in each other's arms, twirling in the warmth of the Sun that streamed down. Then he set her down and looked into her face.*

*"This is farewell, then, my sister."*

*He knew it was; he knew Royaleisia too well to doubt the determination of her nature.*

*"Now we shall all be torn asunder; Strength, Courage,*

and Anger. You shall become mortal; I shall remain Valintara; our brother shall be no more."

"But although there is no future for Afalin, you and I may meet again at the end of time, my brother."

He put his arms around her and kissed her cheek. "I pray that it may be so."

Hours passed and neither moved. At last Royaleisia moved away, and murmured, "I must return to Eloderaý. I had forgotten her, but she will be afraid when she wakes and finds herself alone."

Kanadh stood still, his eyes blank. Then expression returned to them and he looked down at his sister. "She has already awoken; she has been near to a fate worse than death. But she is safe. She is nearing the Council Chamber."

"Then I must go there quickly. Will you come with me, brother?"

His sister's eyes were so grief-filled and pleading that he could not have refused her had he wanted to.

# 20

As Royaleisia and Eloderaý came through the West Gate, they heard a whinnying, and their horses cantered up to them, looking well-fed and rested. They mounted hurriedly, and rode off toward the southwest. Alongside them flowed the Gildan River; they had passed beneath its source whilst they were in the cave. All the way to Gildan Lake they followed the river; then they followed the shoreline of the lake around to the continuation of the Great River, and finally around Malarn Lake until they came in sight of the city of Malarn itself.

Eloderaý gasped as she saw the city. The fires

set the previous night were still burning, and dark smoke rose many feet into the air. In some areas even the flames were high enough to see even from where she and Royaleisia sat on their horses.

Royaleisia looked at the girl grimly.

"Eloderaý, you must obey to the letter every single order which I give you whilst we are in Malarn. Jalavak has taken over the city and I have a duty to discharge. You are to remain in hiding when I go out. Do you understand?"

"Yes," Eloderaý replied. "Only, you said I would play some part in these events. How am I to do so if I am shut up somewhere?"

Royaleisia's brow furrowed slightly. "Trust me, Eloderaý."

She dug her heels into her horse and it started forward. Eloderaý's followed without being told.

It was to the westernmost edge of the city that Royaleisia led. Here in a lush copse of trees thirty yards north of the Malarn Road they tied their horses. Then they proceeded on foot towards the stone wall which encircled the gardens at the back of the palace.

This wall seemed impossible to pass, but Royaleisia appeared to know what she was doing. Staying near to the wall, she went along it until she came to a group of bushes. Here she got down on her hands and knees and crawled straight into the bushes. Eloderaý imitated her, deciding that questions were inappropriate at the moment. Inside the shrubbery, a narrow tunnel, only large enough for a person to slither through on his stomach, led down under the wall. On the other side of the wall they came up behind a hedge of compact greenery, quite thick enough to hide anyone who wished to be concealed. Royaleisia continued to slide along the ground, and Eloderaý continued to follow her lead.

At length they came to a point where the shrubbery ended at the wall of the palace. Now Royaleisia rose to a kneeling position and pushed at one stone. This moved backwards at the touch of her hand, not creaking, completely silently. Beyond the door was darkness, hardly penetrated by the daylight that managed to filter through the bushes. Royaleisia turned, motioned to Eloderaý, and crawled through the doorway. As Eloderaý came through, Royaleisia pushed the stone to, and with that little light gone there was nothing Eloderaý could see anywhere.

Then Royaleisia lit a small torch. In the flickering light Eloderaý could see that they were in a very small room. On the opposite end there was another doorstone, besides which the room was empty.

"We seem to be spending a lot of time underground," she quipped quietly, and Royaleisia smiled. "Where exactly are we?"

"We're below the storerooms of the palace," replied Royaleisia. "Hardly anyone knows about this place, and I believe we are likely the first people to enter it in two hundred years."

"Do you think King Leftar knows about it?"

"I doubt it. This part of the palace was built by the Startern, who love secrets and do not willingly disclose them. Many Startern buildings include secret passages and rooms, for, as they say, who knows when an attack might come? And does that answer satisfy your insatiable curiosity?"

"No, not quite!" Eloderaý answered. "After all, as you say, my curiosity is insatiable! But I will not ask you any more questions now."

"Good, for you should sleep now. I must leave soon to carry out my task."

Eloderaý pulled out her blanket and

attempted to make herself comfortable on the cold flagstones, but then looked up at Royaleisia again. "What is this task of which you speak?"

Royaleisia smiled a second time, but sadly now. "It is not necessary for you to know everything. Go to sleep, Eloderaý."

When Eloderaý awoke, Royaleisia was gone, but she had left a torch burning in a clamp beside the doorstone. Eloderaý had no way of knowing the time, but she knew she was hungry, and she ate a cake of *marcin*, now thoroughly dried out and crumbly. After her meal she settled back against the wall and tried to find something to think about. Wondering what her erstwhile companions were doing now occupied some time, but she could not think about them forever.

She was nodding off again when the doorstone was pulled outwards and a slight figure crept into the room. It was certainly not Royaleisia, and Eloderaý woke up entirely with a start.

"Who are you?"

The figure looked up at her. "Are you Eloderaý?"

"What is it to you?"

"I have a message from Royaleisia. You are to

go at once to the field before the gate of the city, where she will meet you."

Eloderaý suspiciously narrowed her eyes at the small woman. "How am I to know you are not a spy, come to trick me?"

"I cannot prove my identity," replied the stranger. "All you can do is to trust me."

Eloderaý pursed her lips and considered the situation. Surely a spy would have had some token to prove who she was, or who she pretended to be, and not relied on Eloderaý being naïve enough to obey without question. No, this woman must truly be from Royaleisia.

"All right," she said. "I'll come. But I don't know how to get there."

With relief in her expression, the woman nodded. "I'll lead you."

The corridors of the palace and the streets of Malarn were silent and uninhabited, although every now and again a coarse laugh drifted out from some closed chamber or house. But the strange woman seemed unworried by any noise they heard, and led Eloderaý swiftly and surely through the city. As they came near to the east gate of the city the stranger stopped abruptly.

"I must stop here. Royaleisia wishes you to

come unaccompanied."

Before Eloderaý could speak to ask a question or say farewell, the woman had turned and was scuttling away down the street. Feeling suddenly nervous again, but thinking that she may as well continue now, Eloderaý shrugged her shoulders. Then she tiptoed warily through the slightly opened gate and looked around. Although the bodies of those who had fallen in the battle were lying still all round, she could see Royaleisia nowhere.

But she did see the red cloak about the tall man's shoulders, and she recognized him for the Dark Lord.

Unthinking, she took two steps forward, and he must have sensed her there.

"You think to kill me?"

"'Not by the hand of man shall he fall,'" she whispered.

He turned slowly around, a cruel smile on his lips. "And you think that signifies that by the hand of woman he shall fall?"

Overcome by the terror and dread of his countenance, she could not speak to deny it.

"Think not that I have mercy on idiots, nor on children, nor on women." His perpetually blank eyes held hers and seemed to pull her into his well of evil and hate. "You will die as King Kedýran did, without honour, without hope, and alone."

"Not..." She spoke with a great effort. "Not... without... hope..."

"Be silent!" he ordered her.

She fell silent as he bade, but her fingers found their way to the sword of Kanadh. They wrapped themselves about the handgrip, and suddenly she drew the sword. At the touch of the sword against her hand a flood of courage swept through her.

"Not without hope!" she cried. She dove at Jalavak and drove the blade into the flesh of his ankle.

The Dark Lord collapsed onto one knee, screaming at her in his own dark tongue. Gasping for breath, she turned her back on him and tried to walk away, her legs trembling beneath her.

Then something struck her in the back, or seemed to. She crumpled to the ground and the world spun around.

Furiously surveying the woman who had prevented the full power of the death curse from entering Eloderay's body, Jalavak's gaze took on a light of recognition.

"My sister! It has been long since we last met, and I have missed your most delightful presence! But why do I not see in your eyes joy like unto mine at this most happy meeting?" The sarcastic tone suddenly left his voice. "You fear to do battle with me, do you not? You fear to kill me and in your turn lose the life of the Valintari that is in you. You coward, you dare not sacrifice your own immortal life to save a handful of weak men!"

Royaleisia's eyes flashed. "Do you think thus? You will find differently before the Sun sets this day!"

He might have laughed. "The Sun? What Sun? I see no Sun. I have cast it from the sky and all is darkness. I will cast my darkness over all the world. For I am Afalin, Anger, and I am more powerful than you, Royaleisia, *Strength*, pitiful shadow of your own name."

And indeed the Sun was invisible behind a thick layer of black clouds through which no sunlight now penetrated. The world was clothed in darkness but for a red glow which emanated from Jalavak; this light alone prevented utter night.

Royaleisia's glance lingered on the black sky for a few seconds, during which Jalavak's mockingly triumphant eyes fastened on her fair pale face. Then she turned around and dropped onto her knees beside Eloderaý. Placing one hand on his leg, Jalavak pushed himself up from his kneeling position and limped a step closer, his injured foot dragging behind.

"You will give me time for the girl." Royaleisia's statement was an order, and a command from a Valintara countenances no defiance, neither from human nor from fallen Valintara. Jalavak stood motionless, watching her as she bent over Eloderaý's lifeless form.

"*Avsakal fi Afalin Valintara,*" she murmured, "*ranýlratren afh Militer swyh Jalavak li Talna Savamh, rovhinterachwlh wedh sakal lerwnhilh velh Eloderaý. Rývh dagwtwllilh onmýr imlama ledh tiren afh tidhol fi Elamm', li alneh renofh Talna ledh Dwladë fi wledh.*"

As Eloderaý stirred and sucked in a deep breath of air, Royaleisia rose, drawing the Sword from its sheath.

At once Jalavak reached his hand toward her and a visible shock of power shot across the few yards between them. Royaleisia flung up the

Sword before her, and all the power of the curse was pulled into the blade. It ran up and down the metal, hissing and sizzling, till with a bright flash it vaporized. He sent another curse towards her, but this also the Sword sucked into itself. The veins of blood running through the blade began to glow a deep red. A third curse came to the same end, and an indescribable sound rang from the Sword.

Jalavak moved back with a sneer and a laugh. "Have you recovered it, then, sister?"

"Do you cower before it, Afalin?"

In response he attempted the curse a fourth time, yet it too was received into the Sword, which radiated a light that grew brighter and brighter.

"You cannot have the victory over me by use of your dark arts, Afalin. Do battle with me in fairness!"

With a smile Jalavak drew his sword, like a brother to Royaleisia's own: white and gold, and a thing of beauty still, despite its master's fall.

"Yet," he said musingly, lowering his sword, "I hesitate to kill you. For may we not mend our quarrel, Royaleisia, as brother and sister ought, and rule Militer together? Greater power you will have than all living things save myself."

"I do not desire power," she replied, "but rather to submit to the will of Elamm'."

"Then you shall die."

"Indeed I shall!"

For some time they fought, yet neither had the dominion, for they were of equal skill, and in their different ways they were equal in strength. But Jalavak was wounded whilst Royaleisia was fresh, and she gained a slight advantage over him as he tired. At last he made an effort to break through her guard, but the wound dealt him by Eloderaý hampered his attack. He stumbled, and his blade slid until the guard of his sword met the guard of hers. With a twist of her wrist Royaleisia pulled her sword away and cut off his sword arm, nigh to the shoulder.

A flash of white-hot light burst from the Sword of the Star as the blood began to trickle down the blade. The hilt burned painfully hot in Royaleisia's hand, and the Sword shuddered a little. Then the veins of blood within the blade broke free from their trap and ran liquid, mingling with the fresh blood.

The shriek which followed ripped through the air as a knife slashes through silk. Royaleisia fell back, dropping the Sword, blocking her ears. For what seemed like an eternity and more, the scream went on; to those who heard, it seemed to tear apart the foundations of the world.

At last it ended. Jalavak dropped on his face into the dust, and an utter quiet settled over all the earth.

Royaleisia stooped to retrieve the Sword, but as she did so a shock of great pain stabbed through her. She fell beside the body of Jalavak, her bright hair tumbling about her shoulders in the dust. A tearing sensation coursed through her entire body from head to foot, and all that was in her mind became an almost physical torture. As the agony abated she lay spent on the ground.

A flash of light touched Eloderaý's face and she opened her eyes involuntarily. Her back was enveloped with warmth. She turned over painfully, then blinked in the unexpected brightness.

The Sun was shining again.

# 21

LEFT WITHOUT A PURPOSE AS THEIR MASTER'S WILL died, the minions of Jalavak within and without the city fell as one. As they did so, one small cloud scudded over the Sun and blotted out ever so little of its light. Then it hurried away, as though reprimanded by the Sun for its impertinence; the rays of light soared back down to the earth with ever increasing brilliance – yet somehow the eyes of Eloderaý could bear it without hurt. The rays seemed to flicker for a moment; she blinked; when her eyes opened again, all the dead of both armies had disappeared without leaving a trace to mark that they had ever been there. The hair of

Royaleisia, spread across the ground, grew gloriously dazzling, adding to the radiance all around.

A wave of new life swept over the blighted plain, washing away the signs of battle; golden flowers sprung up amongst soft baby grass of a rich green, creating a carpet of royal green and gold. Around the place where Royaleisia lay grew up a garden of lilies and thornless roses, but where the body of Jalavak lay, the ground was blackened and dead, and in later years not the humblest weed would grow there.

The fires in the city were quenched, and the charred remains of homes and shops crumbled into white dust upon the ground. This dust was blown away by a fresh breeze which sprang up and grew into a strong wind that sang rather than howled. The wind's song penetrated everywhere, blowing through windows and doors that stood open to welcome the joy and freedom that was the very air of Militer.

It found its way into the house in Forran where Gonor lay raving and near death, watched over by healers, for the day after Eloderaÿ's escape from Drista, a tall cloaked man had come to Drista and asked that Gonor be handed over to him. None could refuse him, for his voice carried a great authority, and one of the women to who he had spoken said that she might have thought he was a Valintara, so beautiful were his face and voice. But of course that was not possible, she laughed to her friends; and she would have forgotten the incident entirely in a month, had not that beautiful voice haunted all her most joyful dreams for the rest of her life.

The wind blew throughout the house, caressing the faces of the sick. Those who were ill were cured, and those who were wounded were made whole. And when the windsong came to Gonor, it hovered above him for a moment before whisking out the window above his bed. His delirium subsided, and the woman who sat by him started awake, for she had been nodding off a little. She glanced at him, and his sleeping face was peaceful for the first time since he had been brought to Forran.

This same wind blew through the camp of Kanethon outside Forran, where he had escaped with the remnant of his and Fortaer's troops. It stroked the cheeks of Galdore and Tristal, who sat outside their tent whilst Galdore examined a leg wound which his younger brother had received in the midst of the battle.

Tristal raised a hand to feel the wind, and his eyes widened.

"Galdore," he whispered, and Galdore, looking up at him, knew without being told what Tristal meant. He too held up his hand. It was a strong wind; their long hair was whipped up into their faces; but they could feel the very substance of it, and it was soft with a softness they had never known before.

Galdore looked back down at Tristal's leg, and then gave a start. Not a mark was on the leg, where only a moment earlier had been a gaping gash. He stared up at his brother.

"Jalavak?" mouthed Galdore, and at the same time Tristal mouthed, "Royaleisia?"

Tristal leapt up, his leg entirely healed and strong once more. He ran across the camp, shouting for Ringard.

Ringard was sitting despondently in his tent, thinking of his brother, who had died, it seemed, for nothing; he also thought of Leftar, who had been nearly his second father, who had died for the same failed cause. And at the same time he wondered what had kept Royaleisia from the battle even when it was lost.

But when Tristal came near, even the most grief-stricken person could not have ignored the young man's joy-filled yells. Ringard forced himself to rise and leave the tent. Immediately his senses were assailed by the wind, driving his cares from him. And Tristal ran up to him, shouting something which Ringard could not understand. All he could gather was that somehow Tristal's wound was healed, and this he could tell only because the boy was jumping up and down in front of him without a sign of pain.

"The wind, Ringard! Do you feel the wind?"

Ringard could not help but smile at Tristal's enthusiasm. "Who could not?" he laughed, speaking loudly to be heard above the noise of the windsong.

"Do you think it is possible, what I am wondering?"

Not sure what Tristal meant, Ringard glanced up into the boy's eyes. They were gleaming with a kind of excitement that infected anyone who saw it with the same excitement. Suddenly he realized what Tristal was thinking, and a swift hope bounded into his heart.

"In honour of what else would the wind itself

be singing?" he exclaimed.

Now they were both running, running towards King Kanethon's tent. Kanethon was already standing outside the entrance, his face lifted into the wind. He sensed Ringard and Tristal coming toward him, and Galdore had caught up to them by now as well. All four looked at each other, and all four began to laugh. Joy and grief and disbelief were mingled all three into one laugh that rose from the very depths of their souls and rang out across the plain.

When at last they ceased laughing, they each embraced the others, for there was no doubt in their minds that Jalavak was defeated. And then Kanethon gave the order to ride for Malarn, and two hours later, the ragtag remainder of two great armies was strung out along the road leading south from Forran, the King at their head and Galdore, Tristal, and Ringard with Gonor at his side.

Eloderaý knelt by Royaleisia, trying hysterically to knead warmth into the freezing hands that showed no sign of life. Royaleisia seemed hardly to be breathing, although if Eloderaý laid her ear against the other's mouth she could hear and feel a slight movement of the air. It was in this position that she still remained when Kanethon came from Forran and found her kneeling there, despairing of saving Royaleisia. The King himself with Ringard lifted Royaleisia's body onto a makeshift bier and bore her into the city. And Galdore dismounted and raised Eloderaý from the ground. His fair hair glinted in the sunlight and his face was awash in joy; the armour that he wore was stained, yet he appeared as a triumph-ant king. He guided Eloderaý alongside the bier, and she wept bitterly.

The streets were open and empty, for all the Flokav were dead and their bodies gone and the remnants of the destroyed buildings were blown away on the wind. It was not long before they found themselves at the palace, which also was empty but for the flags of Jalavak, which remained where they had been hung. They bore Royaleisia into the great hall, and there they discovered the body of Kedýran lying in the case where Jalavak had laid it to be mocked.

In absolute disbelief of this new tragedy, all

stood immobile and gazed at the body of the dead king. When at last he recovered from the shock, Ringard turned to Galdore who stood beside him, and he dropped onto one knee before the young man.

"I swear to you this day," he spoke, "the allegiance which before I paid to your predecessor Kedýran, and to his predecessor Leftar. I pledge to serve you in all that I do, in all that you justly order, from this hour until the hour of my death, or until the hour in which you release me from your service. This I swear to Galdore King of Fortaer, and may my oath stand before Elamm' and the Valintari until the end of time."

He drew his sword and offered the hilts to Galdore. Galdore simply stared down at Ringard in horror.

"Ringard, what in Militer are you saying?" whispered Tristal.

Kanethon stepped forward and laid a hand on Galdore's shoulder. "Take the sword from Ringard," he instructed him, and as though in a dream, Galdore did so. "Now hold it up, and repeat what I say."

Faltering, Galdore made the reply correctly. "Your allegiance, Ringard son of Frosindal, I accept from you this day. I give to you my thanks for your loyalty to me. May your oath stand before you until the hour of your death, and may death swiftly find you if ever you forget what you have promised to me this day. Now go forth, and may the blessing of Elamm' go with you as you perform my service."

On Kanethon's gesture Galdore returned Ringard's sword to him, and Ringard rose from his knees.

"Now tell me what you have done!" pleaded Galdore, his eyes frightened.

"We will speak in private, my lord King," said Ringard, and jerked his head to indicate that Galdore and his brother alone should come with him and Kanethon.

"What are you playing at?" was Tristal's immediate question when they had settled in a small chamber off a little-used corridor.

Ringard addressed his question to Tristal himself. "Tristal, what was the name of the man who raised you?"

Tristal looked confused. "Why, Garad, but what has he to do with anything?"

"He has little to do with the present matter, but he was not your father."

Tristal jumped up from his seat, furious. "What do you mean, not my father? Stop your game! I do not find you funny!"

"Sit down, Tristal!" ordered Kanethon, and, holding back something else which he seemed about to add, Tristal obeyed. "Hear what Ringard has to say before you speak again."

"If Garad was not our father," said Galdore quietly, "then who was?"

"His name was Kirduil, and he was the twin brother of King Leftar, younger only by a few minutes."

"Eparne's father?" whispered Galdore.

"Eparne was not your brother," replied Ringard, and Tristal emitted an audible sigh. "He was the son of Leftar and Kirduil's younger brother Kedmahl. Your own father died suddenly about a month after Tristal's birth, at the time when Jalavak was rapidly growing in power. It was because his death was so oddly suspicious and because you, Galdore and Tristal, were the next two heirs to the throne that you were hidden with Garad and his wife."

Ringard stopped talking and looked from Galdore to Tristal, his eyes seeming to ask, "Any questions?"

"Our mother," said Galdore suddenly, leaning forward with an intense stare fixed upon Ringard's face. "Is she alive?"

Slowly Ringard shook his head. "She died a couple years after your father."

Galdore frowned, still disbelieving. Then his eyes widened. "When Tristal was lost, when I found him at the palace – the woman with him..."

"No!" cried Tristal of a sudden, and leapt up and began to pace about the room. "You're lying, Ringard. You just want to set my brother up as King so that you'll have a puppet king to control as you see fit. You're lying, you must be lying!"

"Sit *down!*" shouted Kanethon.

"I will not sit down! I refuse to have my brother made a pawn in Staran's manoeuvres! Come back to the Silver Spear, Galdore. We can run our inn in peace now."

But Galdore didn't move, but rather slowly shook his head from side to side. "No. No, Tristal... I believe Ringard."

Tristal stopped pacing and stared down at Galdore. Then he looked at Ringard, who returned the stare with no animosity. For some time he continued to glance back and forth between the two. Finally he sat down again.

"All right," he said. "Galdore can be the King if he wants to. But I'm going back to the Silver Spear. I don't want to be royalty, I'm going to live a free life."

# 22

ROYALEISIA LAY ON A SOFT BED, IN THE MOST beautiful of all the palace gardens – the only gardens which had not been destroyed by the Flokav. But she knew nothing of her rich surroundings. From day to day she slept a deep untroubled sleep. Eloderaẏ sat every day at the side of the cot, watching Royaleisia's sleeping features, which themselves might tell a story, if Eloderaẏ could only discover what it was. When she finally tired of this, Galdore often joined her, and together they read a great many of the books belonging to the King's library. In this way the days passed swiftly, and it was eight days from the day of Jalavak's defeat when Eloderaý was sitting there reading alone, for Galdore must receive the heralds of King Alantar of Gaush, who had come to greet the new King of Fortaer. Eloderaý had her back to Royaleisia and was engrossed in the book, when a voice startled her.

"Who is Kanadh?"

Her head jerked up. This voice she had never heard before: medium in pitch, and slightly rusty as if it had not been used in some time. All details considered, it was a very normal voice, but something lay behind it; confusion and doubt, weariness and age.

She turned around. Royaleisia was awake, sitting up, watching her.

"Who is Kanadh?" she repeated.

It was Royaleisia who had spoken, but it could not have been. For Royaleisia spoke in a song of unearthly beauty. It was Royaleisia who sat before Eloderaý, but it could not be. For Royaleisia had hair of the Sun's radiance. For Royaleisia had eyes which suggested a depth of knowledge that man might not plumb.

"Tell me who Kanadh is," Royaleisia asked a third time. "I dreamt of him time and again whilst I was sleeping, and I cannot think who he might be."

"He... he is a Valintara," Eloderaý replied, "but you know that, Royaleisia! You are also a Valintara!"

Royaleisia laughed a little. "I thank you that you think me so beautiful, Eloderaý – but I am no Valintara."

Something clamped about Eloderaý's heart. Fear. "Royaleisia, do you not remember the Sword of the Star? Do you not remember how you saved us from the dragon? How you led me through the stronghold of the Valintari? How you killed Jalavak?"

"No, child."

Suddenly words came unbidden to Eloderaý's lips. "Your brothers. Kanadh is your brother. Afalin was your brother."

"No, Eloderaý; you are thinking of someone else. I have no brothers."

Eloderaý burst into tears and fled from the garden. Blindly she raced through the palace until she came to the hall where Galdore was speaking with the heralds from Gaush. Heedless of the strangers, she dropped to her knees at his feet and seized his hands.

"What are you doing, Eloderaý?" he growled

softly.

"Royaleisia has woken," she wept, "and she does not remember that she is a Valintara; she remembers nothing that has to do with the Valintari or her place amongst them; she does not even remember her brothers!"

Galdore rose quickly, drawing Eloderaý up with him.

"You will forgive me, my lords," he said to the heralds. "I am urgently called away. You shall be made comfortable until I can return."

Galdore, Tristal, Ringard: each tried all that was in their power to remind Royaleisia of who she was, but she only laughed at them and said they must stop their silliness. Even Gonor failed to bring back her memory. Some things, when mentioned, seemed to remind her of some memory, but the memories never became whole; when this happened it only served to confuse her further. At last they gave up and tried to learn to think of her as the commonplace Fortaeren noblewoman she now seemed to be. Her hair had dulled to a gold not quite as bright as the hair of Galdore and Tristal; her eyes turned to a pale blue. As the rustiness faded from her voice, it became melodious, but not more than another woman's might.

And when the day of Galdore's crowning came, a stranger arrived in Malarn. He kept his hair constantly hidden beneath the hood of his cloak, but one lock often escaped and peeped out, and this lock was brightest gold. His eyes were sea grey, and his tanned hand rested often on the pommel of his sword.

He came to the celebration after the coronation, and greeted the King. As they were speaking together, Royaleisia joined them. The confusion that always surfaced in her eyes when she half-remembered something, wrote itself over her entire face.

"Do I know you?"

He turned to her and smiled, but it was the saddest smile Galdore, watching them, had ever seen.

"No, my lady, I do not think you do."

Her eyes flitted once more across his countenance. "Oh," she said, and turned away.

A few minutes later, the man took his leave of Galdore and mingled with the other guests, and suddenly Eloderaý saw him and recognised him. And she was so bewildered by the change in Royaleisia, that she entirely forgot her awe and fear of the Valintara, and, dashing forward, caught his hands in hers.

"Explain it to me!" she demanded.

He asked her nothing, did not rebuke her, but led her to a quiet corner outside the great hall.

"Why, my lord? Why does she remember nothing?"

"Since the day when Afalin was banished it was ordained. Royaleisia's Sacrifice, it was named that day; that she would complete what she began. But when a Valintara kills, he is cast from our number and becomes mortal. So it was with Afalin; so it is with Royaleisia. Sixteen of us there were in the days when the world was young; fourteen there remain."

"But he at least kept his memories!"

"It is Royaleisia's Sacrifice," Kanadh repeated. "Afalin killed no Valintara, but Royaleisia did. Any Valintara who kills is cast out, but one Valintara who kills another loses everything. Royaleisia shall live a year from the day when she killed Afalin. No more than a year; no less than a year."

Eloderaý backed away, raised her gaze to his face, saw her grief, too great for tears, mirrored even more greatly in him.

# 23

ELODERAÝ REFUSED TO ACCOMPANY THE KING TO Gaush when he brought Gonor back to his old home; she wanted to stay near Royaleisia every moment she could spare. Tristal, however, agreed to leave his inn and go with them – but only because he wished to say a last goodbye to the old man, with whom he had become good friends. Gonor's madness had completely left him, and he conversed lucidly on many topics, but he constantly avoided the subject of his family, his life in Gaush, and his imprisonment by Jalavak. The only mention he had made of Gaush was a request that he be allowed to return there to end his life in the land he loved.

They took the Malarn Road north. It was flanked by fields bursting with joyful new life, and numerous flowers were discovered that no man had ever seen before. One day they had stopped for the night when Gonor went out looking for water; he found a meadow filled with a new flower that had not yet been noticed by anyone in the company. It grew delicately on a pale green stem which grew perhaps three inches high before it widened out into a tiny green blossom only a little darker in hue than the stem itself. This flower absolutely captivated Gonor, and Tristal had to come and find him when it was time for supper.

The old man was crouching in the meadow, carefully avoiding crushing any of the blooms. His eyes were fixed on one flower. Tristal knelt down beside him.

"Look how perfect it is," Gonor whispered, not taking his eyes from the flower. "Could I name this one, do you think?"

"For certain," replied Tristal.

"Then I name it for my wife. It reminds me of her. She was so slender and delicate, at times I thought she might blow away. She was so beautiful, my Wynna. Do you know, Tristal, I used to believe she might be a Valintara? She used to lie in the grass and watch me work, and sometimes I couldn't even see her when I looked her way. She would wear green dresses, just the colour of this flower, with a grass-green girdle about her waist, and her flaxen hair caught up in a green ribbon. Will you tell the King I name this flower for Wynna, Tristal? But don't pick any; bring him here and show him, but don't let him pick any either. Leave them all green and growing where they belong."

The Old West Road took them to Milltam, the largest city in Gaush – which was not a great distinction, for there were only three cities in the land. Gonor's old home was a day's journey from Milltam, a mile or two out of a poor mountain village called Eadfell.

Gonor became more and more cheerful as they neared the village, and as they entered Eadfell he became almost wild with excitement, realizing how little the place had changed in the fifty-three years since he had been kidnapped by Jalavak. As they passed by the blacksmith's forge, Gonor uttered a gasp and ran toward to the smith within, a young lad in his early twenties.

"Restac!" he cried eagerly.

The young man looked up. "*Hana-gawë*, my friend!" he called. "Are you looking for my father?"

Gonor slowed. "You are not Restac? But you look exactly like him."

"I'm his son; Sestimon is my name. My father is at home if you wish to see him. Since he grew old he does not come to the forge anymore. But you need only go next door to find him. He has nothing to do all day and will be happy to see you, I'm sure, if you're an old friend of his." Sestimon waved his hand at a poor but well-kept cottage next to the forge.

"*Samach ne*," said Gonor, and turned back to his companions. His excitement was slightly quenched. "They'll all be old now," he said to Tristal. "I had forgotten."

"Go visit your friend," Tristal replied. "We'll wait in the road."

Gonor nodded. "I will not take too long," he told Galdore, and knocked on the door of the cottage. In a moment the door opened, Gonor disappeared within, and all was quiet outside.

Gonor had said he would not be long, but sunset was only a few hours away by the time he came out again. Galdore, Tristal, and Ringard were sitting patiently against the wall of the cottage; the twelve soldiers who had accompanied the group had been dismissed by Galdore and had since found the inn.

The two miles through thick woods to Gonor's lonely cottage were crossed quickly. Gonor would allow no delay. After half an hour they came out into a large clearing in the middle of which stood the house. Ivy was grown up all around it, plugging up the windows. The thatch of the roof was rotted completely away and only rotting beams remained to tell of the roof that had been there half a century before. A wooden door hung crooked on one hinge.

Gonor showed no disappointment at the state of his home. He seemed delighted to see it once more, in any condition. Slipping through the crack between the door and wall, he moved back and forth, back and forth, between the two rooms. They too were choked up with weeds and ivy, but clearly Gonor recognised everything that was visible among the growth. He righted a table that lay knocked on its side...

He jumped up to pull out her chair as she set the dish on the table, and she sat down, laughing at him.

"I might think you were practising to be a king someday, the way you always treat me like a queen," she teased him gently.

"You are my queen," he said from behind her, and kissed the top of her head. Then he picked up Armald. "And you are my little prince!" He tossed the toddler into the air, and Armald came down again into his father's arms with a shriek of excitement. "Now into your chair you go, my lord the prince."

He set Armald in his chair, pushed it towards the table, then seated himself last. The family began their meal. It was a delicious stew of vegetables, beef, and herbs from Wynna's garden in back of the cottage, and Gonor intended to stuff himself on his favourite dish. He had finished one bowl and was beginning a second when something thudded against the door.

Wynna looked up. "Come in!"

Instead of opening outwards, however, the door burst inwards. Red-clad creatures, sunburnt to a crispy perfection, overran the tiny room. The heavy oaken table went over with a crash, and stew splattered everywhere. Wynna was screaming and clutching Armald; the baby was silent, watching the commotion with enormous blue eyes.

With a start Gonor came back to the present and found his three friends watching him. He moistened his dry lips and tried to smile.

"It's nothing."

He bent down again and picked up a corroded salver and set it in the middle of the table...

*"Look, Gonor – look what I got!"*

*Wynna dashed around the corner of the house and Gonor straightened, tossing away a weed and swiping the soil from his hands and knees. His wife was carrying a platter of some sort, shiny and bright. He reached out and touched it carefully with a fingertip.*

*"It must have cost you a denhl at least!"*

*"It was only ten pennies!"*

*He couldn't believe that. Why, the dish must be pure copper from the look of it, glazed over with some finish he didn't recognize, to make it safe for holding food.* "From whom did you buy it?"

*"Oh, Restac's father was clearing out a lot of old stuff he had in his cottage, and he was selling some of it in the market for right low prices. I couldn't bear to leave it, it was so shiny. Isn't it beautiful, Gonor?"*

*He had to agree – especially when it was filled with*

*stew and the glints of copper shone through as you ran a*
*spoon through the stew. It was certainly a beautiful dish.*
*But his wife's laughing eyes were more captivating still.*

This time his friends were carefully looking the other way when Gonor recovered, and without speaking the old man dropped down into the weeds and began to dig among them for the chairs. But they were long rotted, and all he could find were a few pieces, driven through with rusty nails that proved that the wood had once been part of a chair. He had been so proud of those chairs when they were new. Every stick of wood he himself had cut to the perfect shape and size; every single nail he had paid for at the forge even though Restac wanted to give them to him as a gift. All that was left of them now was aged and broken – like himself. He stood up.

"I'm going outside," he said, "and I would like to be alone." There was a pause as the other three men watched him and he them. "I don't know exactly what to say," he continued at last. "Royaleisia told me back on the Matren Pass that my labours would end soon. I..." He swallowed. "You have been kind to me, and you are my good friends. But Wynna is calling me back to her."

He walked forward and briefly embraced

each of them.

"*Sariënh, redhini amh* – farewell, my friends."

Still not one of them spoke, but Tristal was crying and tears stood in Galdore's and Ringard's eyes. Then Gonor turned from them and went out the door.

He crossed the yard and bypassed a lone fencepost that told where the boundary of the meadow had been, fifty-three years past. The meadow was beautiful, beautiful in the springtime. As he came to the middle of the meadow he espied something familiar in the grass. He bent down and gently touched a pale green flower.

"They grow here too now," he whispered. "Here in her favourite place."

He lowered his face and kissed the top of the Wynna-flower. He was so tired, so terribly tired, and the flower smelled so sweet; it smelled like Wynna's hair when she had woven it with flowers. Maybe if he waited here for long enough, Wynna would find him. This was where she loved most to be. He lay down on the ground and closed his eyes, and it was so wonderful to lie there and rest. His thoughts faded and the wind bore them far, far away.

*When he woke he found himself in an unfamiliar place, but he felt as though this was home. And before him stood the slight figure of a woman, dressed in green with long light yellow curls running wild down her back. Gonor rose to his feet. The woman stretched out a hand towards him, and then they were running toward each other, and he had found her, his Wynna, unchanged though he had grown old, and now he would never lose her again. Then Gonor saw him. A child, running through the grass, and tripping on a root and falling to the ground. "Dada!" he cried, and picking himself up lurched into his father's arms.*

*And then as the family embraced each other a light grew in the distance and came nearer, nearer, until it would have blinded a mortal. And a figure stepped out of the light, and Gonor was struck with fearful awe...*

# 24

Malarn was rebuilt in more loveliness than ever before, for the original buildings were now gone and King Galdore had ordered the city rebuilt with houses that had gardens, bright cheery gardens. The streets were wide and bright, and everyone you passed walking down the road would greet you with real welcome, for the rebirth of Militer still infected the hearts of all with joy.

Even Serpent's Road was resurrected, and the Silver Spear rebuilt, and the proprietor of the inn, Tristal the brother of the King, served meals that were renowned as the best in Fortaer.

Oftentimes of an evening a cloaked figure would come in for supper and order chicken and ale, and when Tristal's work was done he would join the guest; and the two would have an ale together and talk for hours.

It was a year less a day from the defeat of Jalavak, and the Queen of Fortaer walked in the vibrant meadows before the gate of Malarn. A small red-haired baby girl laughed in the arms of her mother's friend, tall and beautiful. From a distance she seemed a girl of twenty – not much older than the Queen herself – but if one looked closely into the woman's face, it was clear that she was aged, aged near the point of dotage. Yet her wits were clearly all about her, for she laughed and joked with the Queen. But the Queen was silent and sad.

Of a sudden Eloderaý came out of her reverie and looked up at Royaleisia, and Royaleisia was staring at her strangely.

"What?" she asked, trying to cheer herself.

"Do you want to visit the stronghold, Eloderaý?"

"The... *stronghold*?"

"Yes – do you not remember? There you met my brother; there Eparne nearly killed you."

"Of course I remember, but do *you* remember?

"Why should I not?"

Eloderaẏ felt joy rise up in her. "We cannot bring Elriel with us; I'll have to bring her back to her nurse."

She retrieved her small daughter from Royaleisia, and ran back to the gate where a pretty young woman stood.

"Kaaria, I'm riding out with Royaleisia. Take Elriel back to the palace, and tell the King where I am going."

She motioned to a man who stood aside holding the bridles of two horses; he brought them forward to meet Eloderaẏ, who was joined by Royaleisia just then. The two women mounted their horses and rode off eastward.

The whole remainder of the day they spent in exploring the Valintari stronghold, and Royaleisia had remembered all that she had forgotten. Hope sprung into Eloderaẏ's heart that Royaleisia would not die after all come the following day, that she had been received back into the number of the Valintari for her faithful sacrifice; but no, no outward change came over Royaleisia. Her voice, eyes, hair; all remained the same as they had been for a year.

Then this was Royaleisia's reward: not life, but memory.

When they returned to Malarn, Royaleisia was happier than Eloderaý had ever before seen her. She was not solemnly glad in the manner of a Valintara, for she was mortal now. Nor was she merry in the manner of a human. A quiet joy radiated from her, and she seemed absolutely content; and for the first time Eloderaý felt that perhaps she could bear the day that inevitably approached, second by second becoming closer.

Tristal came that night to see his brother and his wife, and Ringard with him. The five sat up very late, recalling their adventures. It was after midnight when they finally went to bed, yet they woke some time before dawn and were refreshed and not weary from lack of sleep.

Morning came, but the sky stayed dark: deep blue studded with all the stars. Yet the Sun too rose in unbearable brightness; its light did not spread over the earth, however, but remained in one place, and the light was white: the Sun took its place as a common star.

Galdore and Eloderaý stood side by side on a balcony, watching the sky, and finding the constellations to distract them from what lay ahead. One by one they picked out the stars of the Silisik, the Jogen, the Mountains, and Elharoýal – the Mystery of the Sky. Then they searched for the Valintari constellations, Ralẃk, Tarna, and Talna. But search where they would, they could not find Afalin, the fifth star of Ralẃk; and, below where Afalin should have been, the light of the star Royaleisia throbbed brightly but erratically.

Neither spoke in words, but their eyes communicated with each other. Galdore's eyes said, *Where is Royaleisia?* and Eloderaý's frantically replied, *Find her!* Then Ringard and Tristal joined them and gestured towards the east. Galdore looked out again over the city, and he gasped and Eloderaý turned to see what he saw.

Royaleisia stood on the plain before the city, and her arms were raised toward the sky. Her star was hovering above her, and it was pulsing madly, emitting a light so bright that it rivalled that of the sun. The woman's stature seemed to increase until she towered above the ground. In the starlight her hair glinted and sparkled, returned to its old storm of colour. She was clad in a simple white gown, and she looked like a queen, great and wise and lovely.

And then the star was singing.

It sang a song that was great and clear, heartrending and pure, so lovely that men might die for it. And the hearts of those who heard the star's song were filled with an ache of intense longing, longing for something they did not know but felt they should and, someday, would know.

Who may describe the Song of Royaleisia? What words of men could pay just homage to this song of unearthly beauty? And who might say how long it lasted? It might have been a minute, or an hour, or a year, or a century. But as a final pure note died away, the song ended. Then the star at last ceased its throbbing, and it hung motionless in the sky as though resting from its exertion. Slowly the brightness faded from it and it became again as a normal star, but those on the balcony were unable to pull their eyes from it.

Hours passed and not a breath of air moved. Still Ringard, Galdore, Tristal, and Eloderaý watched the star of Royaleisia.

It remained utterly still.

Then it flickered and went out.

CONTINUE READING
FOR A PREVIEW

# SEA OF CRYSTAL
# SEA OF GLASS

## BY BENITA J. PRINS

# 1

# BE NOT AFRAID

One moment the skies were clear; the next, rain fled from them in terrified haste. Einur raced for his cave shelter, leaving his sheep, undisturbed by the downpour, still ripping up grass. Reaching the cave, he crouched just inside, shivering – already drenched despite his swift retreat from the open field.

As his shivers subsided, he raised his fingers to his mouth and blew a shrill whistle. Presently there came the beat of wings, and a dark form alighted beyond the cave opening.

"Come here, Efrix," commanded Einur, and the dragon slithered in. His body fit snugly within the stone walls; he was a small specimen of his kind.

"Einur?" came a second voice from outside.

"Is that you, Gernhr?"

"Einur!" Gernhr's voice was filled with terror. "You must come at once!"

Einur's heart nearly stopped.

*Lody.*

"Move!" he snapped at Efrix, shoving at the dragon's scaly side with his hands. Slowly the creature wedged himself back out, Einur impatient with fear behind him.

"Have they taken Lody?" he shouted, taking hold of Gernhr's shoulders and shaking his friend. "Where is she?"

Gernhr broke free and shook his head, trying to catch his breath. "No, no, Einur, not Lody. Einur, *your* name was drawn!"

Einur's mind froze in relief at Gernhr's initial reassurance, the latter part of his statement not registering at once. Then it filtered through.

"*My* name?"

The thought of this happening had never once occurred to the boy. Rather, the possibility which had haunted him ever since his little sister's birth was that she would be chosen, that she would be taken to the Temple from where no child had ever returned. That Lody would be sacrificed to the Great Achiel.

*Not me.*

Gernhr was watching him when the dizzy blackness faded from his vision. "You know what we planned if Lody was chosen, Einur. It's little different now it's you instead of her. You can run off, Einur, live in the wild somewhere. I'll even come with you, if you want me to."

He broke off and stared at Einur, whose eyes were glassy and confused.

"You aren't going with the Illyrië, are you?"

Einur revived himself. "I'll leave right now. But you mustn't come with me; your dad needs you. Your ma will take care of Lody, no?"

Gernhr nodded. Then he tensed.

"They're coming!"

Einur stood still for three seconds, but he did not have Gernhr's swift hearing.

"Run! They've tracked you here!"

"Efrix!" called Einur, and quickly embraced his friend. "Goodbye, Gernhr. Tell Lody I love her, and I'll come back as soon as I can."

He jumped onto Efrix's back and exclaimed, "Go!"

The dragon didn't move. Einur repeated his order once, twice, panic leaping into his voice.

"What are you doing, Einur? Go!" shouted Gernhr.

Einur glanced behind him; the hirelings of the Illyrië were in sight now, coming over a small hillock. There were ten or so, perhaps fifteen. Einur kicked Efrix hard in the sides.

"Go, you stupid creature!"

Still Efrix remained on the ground.

"Just leave him and run!"

The pursuers were only a few hundred feet away. Einur gave them one look and slipped off Efrix's back, running now for dear life up into the bracken. His path led him up the side of a small mountain, yet his pace slowed not at all. The yells of his enemies were close behind him – with every step he took, he expected to be yanked back. Gradually, however, the shouts grew further away, and then died out altogether. Einur allowed himself one brief pause and looked down the mountainside. His would-be captors had become worn out by the race up the steep slope, and had retreated. He couldn't see Gernhr anymore; please the Great Achiel he was unharmed.

*But won't the Great Achiel be enraged that he helped the sacrifice escape?* he thought. Yet he could do nothing but turn and go on.

His steps soon became stumbling, and presently rest was imperative. If only Efrix hadn't been so stubborn, Einur could've ridden on him instead. But what a ridiculous thing for the dragon to suddenly do! Why, everyone used dragons as their mounts; the creatures were bred for that very purpose!

The dragon himself landed beside Einur just then.

"You wicked creature!" the boy told it, and it snorted and nuzzled its snout up against his shoulder. He gave it a slap and repeated his admonishment, but the slap was gentle and the rebuke no harsher.

They settled into positions as comfortable as the rain-soaked ground and Einur's wet clothes allowed. Einur still made a pretence of being angry; but Efrix let out periodic soft snorts until his master rubbed the top of his scaly head and laughed, "You ought to be ashamed of yourself!"

They went to sleep with Einur snuggled against Efrix's warm side.

Einur woke early to find Efrix again gone but the sun returned. As he waited for Efrix to come back – as he was sure the dragon would – he breakfasted off henla, a type of leaf that grew year-round and was very nourishing. The flavour was slightly tart, making the leaves an invigorating morning meal. He was finishing his breakfast when Efrix arrived.

"Where did you go?" he asked, rubbing his hand up and down Efrix's back. "Have you found breakfast? Good, let's go!"

He climbed onto Efrix and the dragon lifted off. The day was beautiful; there wasn't a cloud anywhere in the azure sky, and a light breeze blew Einur's blond hair off his shoulders.

The sun showed it was little past noon when they alighted to find some sort of dinner. Einur found nothing but more henla leaves; he ate these whilst Efrix flew off to look for his own dinner.

He woke from a brief nap feeling delightfully warm and extremely relaxed. Through his still-closed eyelids the sunlight streamed into his mind, and he drank it in lazily. Then something blocked the light, and irritably he opened his eyes to see what had happened.

Over him, staring down into his face, stood a man, his hair and beard pale green, and his eyes sea-blue. He wore forest-green robes and carried a long staff engraved with the recurring motif of a fish.

"Einur, is it not?"

Einur scrambled onto his feet. "How do you know my name?"

"I have my sources," replied the man. "And as I do know it, in fairness I should give you mine. I am Eigion, and some of what I know, you must learn."

"Learn what?"

"What you must know to perform your task."

Without realising it, Einur was backing away from the stranger ever so gradually. "What task?"

"Stop moving!" commanded Eigion, and abruptly Einur noticed his slight movements backward and stopped. "Sit, and I will explain everything to you."

Einur sat in obedience, and Eigion seated himself facing the boy. He laid his staff on the ground beside him and drummed on his cheek with long fingers, his eyes keenly taking in everything observable about Einur. Einur flushed and scowled.

"I haven't got all the time in the world. If you have something to tell me, you had better do it quickly."

A smile darted across Eigion's lips. "You should do well," he said cryptically. "Are you a follower of the cult of the Great Achiel?"

"Of course," muttered Einur, but the hatred in his eyes gave the lie to his words.

"Despite your attempt to conceal it, you hate the cult and all that goes with it. Do you not?"

Einur's glance jumped up to meet Eigion's, then descended again to the ground. He did not reply.

"Do you not?"

Einur was still silent, but Eigion did not look away from him.

"Do you need me to answer?" Einur said at last.

"I know what your answer is, yes, but I do need you to tell me yourself."

"Why?"

"Why do you not wish to answer me?"

"Oh, all right. Yes, I hate the Great Achiel, and I hate the Illyrië, and the whole business. Now you can execute me. That's what you want, after all."

Eigion smiled, a genuine smile. "That was the thing furthest from my mind."

"What was closer, then?" Einur was still argumentative in his tones, but he could not deny to himself that he was interested in this man – or whatever he was – greatly interested. He wanted to know of what task Eigion spoke, and against his wishes he began to believe that Eigion was probably on his side... *Side? Where did that idea come from?*

"Although you hate it, do you believe in its truth?"

It was a question Einur had never considered in his sixteen years, and it gave him pause. Finally he answered, "Yes."

"Why?"

He was honest. "I've no idea."

"Give it up."

Einur might have hated the cult and wished to leave it, but still he was shocked at the blunt words that suggested such a thing. "*Give it up?*"

"So I said."

"But why?"

"So many questions! Not only have you no

conviction in your belief, but had you, it were wrongly placed. There is truth in the cult of Achiel only in the sense that there is at least a seed of truth in everything; besides this, there is only evil." He held up his hand to prevent Einur's open mouth from generating a horrified response to his disrespect of the Great Achiel's name. "No more questions, Einur Landman! Listen now, and question after. For what I have just stated is the basis of your task.

"I will begin my story far back in the history of Kelyan. Precisely five thousand years after the creation of the world, the Second Tribe of Lo'Rien rebelled against the Master of the Kelyanic Harmony, creating their own demonic cult worship, the very one to which men yet hold this very day. The First Tribe also succumbed to the evil spread by the Second Tribe, but the Third Tribe refused to join with the others. Battle was joined between the Tribes; the First and Second were victorious, and the remnants of the Third escaped into... well, into oblivion."

"Doesn't anyone know where they went?" exclaimed Einur before Eigion could continue.

The older man shook his head.

"Is my task to find them?" Einur was curiously

intrigued by Eigion's tale, and the mystery of the lost Tribe called to him somehow.

"Partly."

Einur repressed a cheer. "What else?"

"Listen." The rebuke was impressively gentle, but it completely quenched Einur's eagerness. "Unless it is checked, the cult of the Great Achiel will continue to grow in evil, as it has for the past five thousand years. However, it cannot be checked, except by one means."

Again excitement surged from Einur's heart to his throat. "How?"

Eigion did not answer his question directly. "The first part of your task is to find the lost Third Tribe; more precisely, to find their king. That is the easy part."

Certainly Einur was excited about this quest, yet he gulped now. "That's the easy part? They've been lost for five thousand years and that's the *easy* part?"

"The second part is more vague. The fall of the cult can be caused only by a sacrifice made by one person."

"What kind of sacrifice?" Visions of the culture of human sacrifice in which he'd grown up flitted through the young man's head, and he thought of his little sister.

"That is unknown." Seeming to sense the uncertainty now tormenting Einur, he added, "But it is not of the kind of which you are thinking."

"So I'm supposed to find this tribe that's been lost practically since the beginning of time, and then someone's supposed to make a sacrifice that no one knows any details of."

"I am glad to see that you have absorbed my instructions so well."

Einur sat silently for some time. *If I do this, I supposedly have a chance of getting rid of the danger to Lody... if they don't draw her name whilst I'm gone, which is actually quite likely, considering they probably cheat at the drawing... But this quest thing is such a ridiculous idea! Yet if there's a possibility of giving Lody better chances of surviving her ninth year... What else am I going to do with myself anyway? I can't go back home now, and it can't really hurt me much to go journeying all over Kelyan. And really, I'd do anything to destroy something that might hurt Lody. Doesn't hurt that it's an evil cult either.*

"I'll go."

Eigion nodded. "Do you trust me?"

"Yes."

"No, Einur. Do you trust me?"

Confused, Einur repeated his answer.

"Einur! It is not enough to *say* you trust me. You must *trust* me. Think about it first, as you did about accepting your task. I do not wish you to take this lightly. You *must not* take this lightly."

Again Einur sat in thought. Yes, he trusted Eigion – to a human degree at least. True, the man was unlike anyone he'd ever met, but this somehow didn't decrease his trust, instead increasing it; few of the people in Einur's life had been worthy of trust, and the differences between the Illyrië and Eigion attracted him. Besides this, there was also an aura about Eigion which spoke of something much greater than the man.

He was about to tell Eigion this when Efrix returned, alighting close beside his master. The dragon observed Eigion with as much suspicion as a dumb creature can gather. Efrix seemed to shrink from the stranger, and if dragons had had the capacity to fear man, Einur would have said that without a doubt, his dragon was terrified of Eigion.

Eigion was frowning. "That is your dragon, if I am not mistaken."

Einur nodded briefly, but changed the subject

back to the previous one. "I do trust you, sir, with all my heart."

"Are you willing to prove it?"

Confused, Einur blinked. "Yes?" he almost questioned.

Eigion unbuckled something from around his waist and held it out to Einur: a long sword in a plain leather scabbard.

"Take it."

Einur took it, his stomach suddenly alive with nervousness.

"Now kill the dragon."

He nearly dropped the sword. "Kill *Efrix*?"

Eigion only stared at him.

"But he's my mount, he's my friend!"

"On your quest against evil, no dragon is a friend of yours. Did you not say that you trust me?"

Slowly, Einur turned to Efrix. Efrix – yes, it was Efrix, but at the same time it was not Efrix. The dragon's coal-black eyes were turning red, and its chest blazed orange: the latter a clear sign of anger, the former a phenomenon Einur had never seen in a dragon.

Then Efrix spoke.

"If you kill me, you too will find death."

Einur shrieked aloud.

"If you kill me, you will find despair."

Einur continued to scream.

"If you kill me, you will find oblivion."

"Enough!"

It was Eigion's voice, but deeper and richer than before, and it quieted the dragon for a moment. Efrix turned his eyes to Eigion, and seemed no longer afraid of the man but contemptuous.

"And as for you, you fool..."

"Enough, foul creature!" Eigion cried again. "Einur, kill him now!"

Trembling uncontrollably, Einur stooped and raised the sword, which he had dropped when Efrix first spoke. The fingers of his right hand wrapped convulsively around the hilts, he faced what had been his dragon – and now seemed to be so once more. Efrix's eyes were again a normal black, and his chest silver-grey like the rest of his scales. Despite what Einur had just witnessed, a doubt filled his mind. Had it not been but a dream?

*Did you not say that you trust me?*

He looked towards Eigion, who now did or said nothing to influence the young man's decision. He looked back at Efrix, who gazed at him with his familiar, submissive, friendly gaze.

*Did you not say that you trust me?*

A sudden conviction filled Einur, a conviction that by distrusting Eigion, he distrusted something – or someone – far greater. He raised the sword... and drove it with all his might into Efrix's neck.

# AVAILABLE NOW

# ABOUT THE AUTHOR

Benita J. Prins has been writing since she was six years old. Her imagination likes to work over time, and this is at the root of her love for fantasy. She loves to be inventing and feels at a loss when she doesn't have a fantasy location to flesh out. When not writing, Benita keeps busy with music, graphic design, and increasing her already enormous book collection. Some of her favourite authors are J.R.R. Tolkien, C.S. Lewis, Michael O'Brien, John Buchan, and Jane Austen.

Benita lives in southwestern Ontario, Canada.

Instagram: @benitajprinsauthor

## BY THE SAME AUTHOR

*Sea of Crystal, Sea of Glass*
(previously published as *Seascape*)

*Aratar, Peredhil, and Halflings, Oh My!:*
*The Ultimate Tolkien Quiz*